World Book Myths & Legends Series

NORTH AMERICAN MYTHS & LEGENDS

AS TOLD BY PHILIP ARDAGH

ILLUSTRATED BY OLIVIA RAYNER

MYTH OR LEGEND?	2
NATIVE NORTH AMERICANS	4
TALES OF THE GREAT HARE	7
THE QUEST FOR HEALING	11
THE CRYING THAT DEFEATED A GOD	17
BLACK BIRD, BRIGHT SKIES	21
THE CURSE OF THE SNAKE'S MEAT	25
THE GIANT OF THE LOGGING CAMPS	27
THE MAN WHO PLANTED TREES	30
KING OF THE WILD FRONTIER	32
MAMA AND THE HAIRY MAN	35
BRER RABBIT AND THE TAR BABY	38
WHEN PEOPLE HAD WINGS	40
COYOTE AND THE STORY OF DEATH	43
MYTHS AND LEGENDS RESOURCES	48
WHO'S WHO IN MYTHS AND LEGENDS	53
MYTHS AND LEGENDS GLOSSARY	58
CUMULATIVE INDEX TO MYTHS & LEGENDS SERIES	60

World Book, Inc.
a Scott Fetzer company
Chicago

MYTH OR LEGEND?

Long before people could read or write, stories were passed on by word of mouth. Every time they were told, they changed a little, with a new character added here and a twist to the plot there. From these ever-changing tales, myths and legends were born.

WHAT IS A MYTH?

In early times, people developed stories to explain local customs and natural phenomena, including how the world and humanity developed. These myths were considered sacred and true. Most include superhuman beings. Many North American myths include gods who can turn themselves into animals.

WHAT IS A LEGEND?

A legend is very much like a myth. The difference is that a legend is often based on an event that really happened or a person who really existed in relatively recent times.

NORTH AMERICAN PEOPLES

The myths and legends in this book come from three very different North American peoples: Native North Americans, European settlers, and African Americans.

NATIVE NORTH AMERICANS

Native North Americans, who were called "Indians" by the Europeans, were the first people to live in North America. They walked from Asia about 25,000 years ago when the two continents were linked by ice. They formed many different groups. You can find out more about these groups on pages 4 and 5.

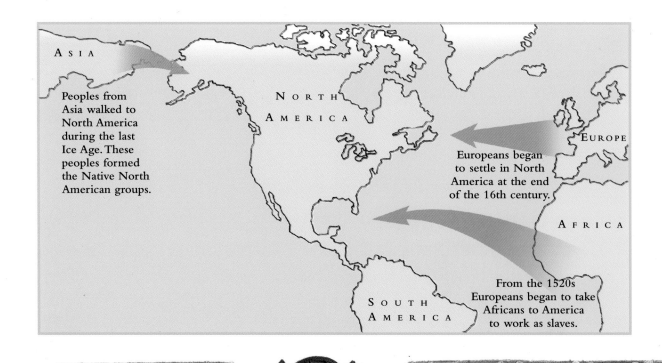

ASIA

Peoples from Asia walked to North America during the last Ice Age. These peoples formed the Native North American groups.

NORTH AMERICA

EUROPE

Europeans began to settle in North America at the end of the 16th century.

AFRICA

From the 1520s Europeans began to take Africans to America to work as slaves.

SOUTH AMERICA

EUROPEAN SETTLERS

The Vikings arrived in North America about 1,000 years ago, but the first Europeans to stay and build their homes there arrived about 100 years after Christopher Columbus discovered San Salvador in 1492. Most of these early settlers lived on the east coast. It was not until the 19th century that people began to move west and to settle in the rest of North America.

AFRICAN AMERICANS

African Americans were originally brought to North America by the Europeans to work as slaves on tobacco plantations. This terrible trade in humans continued until 1865 when slavery was finally abolished.

LIVING MYTHS AND LEGENDS

Native American myths and legends are very much alive and are still told today. They are an important part of the cultures of the various groups and are used in art and religious ceremonies. It is important to remember that what one person might see as a myth or legend, another might see as a part of his or her religion.

HOW DO WE KNOW?

In the 18th and 19th centuries, a number of Europeans visited the Native North American groups and recorded their way of life, including their myths and legends. The stories retold in this book are based on some of these early written accounts.

LATER MYTHS AND LEGENDS

The European and African American stories are far more recent. Most were retold by the 19th-century European settlers and their African slaves. Like the Native American myths and legends before them, these tales were originally passed on by word of mouth and were only later written down. And they are still changing as they are retold today. Many African American stories–first told in North America by slaves–have their roots in African myths and legends, but were adapted to fit this new life far away from home.

NOTE FROM THE AUTHOR

Myths and legends from different cultures were told in very different ways. The purpose of this book is to tell *versions* of these stories, but not to try to copy the way in which they were actually told. I hope that you enjoy them and this book will want to make you find out more about the lives of the different North American peoples, as well as their myths and legends.

NATIVE NORTH AMERICANS

Native North American groups were scattered right across North America–from the Canadian Inuit in the north to the Calusa in what is now southern Florida. The term *Native North Americans* includes many different peoples with different beliefs and ideas. Some are grouped together by a shared language, such as the Algonquian-speaking peoples who are made up of over ten groups.

SHARED BELIEFS

Native North American groups share many beliefs, even though their ways of life and their myths and legends may be different. A common belief is that everything on earth is somehow connected–every plant, every animal, every person, every speck of dirt or drop of water. Harming something for no good reason will upset the balance of nature and will, in the end, harm everything else.

SHARED MYTHS

Both the Cherokees and the Creeks have a myth that tells how bears were once a human group. According to this myth, when food became scarce, the bears went into the forest and returned as "hairy humans." They offered to be hunted by the others for their meat and skins. This was their sacrifice so that the others could survive. This is also why the Cherokees and Creeks say that you must always respect what you hunt.

COMMON THEMES

There are other common themes in Native North American myths and legends. Many myths about the creation of the earth include a flood, and a number of different groups have stories about a coyote and a hare as mischievous trickster gods. The shaman–part doctor and part priest–is an important member of some Native American communities and appears in many of their myths and legends.

LOST HOMELANDS

Over time, as their land has been populated by settlers from overseas, many Native North Americans have lost their traditional homelands. Large numbers were resettled on reservations but still have strong ties with their land. Between the arrival of European settlers in the late 1500s and 1900, the Native North American population dropped from about one million to a few hundred thousand.

ARCTIC

SUBARCTIC

NORTHWEST
COAST

PLATEAU

GREAT BASIN

CALIFORNIA

PLAINS

NORTHEAST

SOUTHEAST

SOUTHWEST

This map shows the "culture areas" of the various Native North American groups. Each culture area, representing a number of groups with a similar way of life, is shown in a different color.

KEY TO THE VARIOUS GROUPS

Arctic groups include:
Inuit, Netsilik, and Aleut

Subarctic groups include:
Cree, Naskapi, Ingalik, and Beaver

Northwest Coast groups include:
Chinook, Haida, and Nootka

Plateau groups include:
Shuswap, Nez Percé, and Yakima

Plains groups include:
Sioux, Comanche, Blackfoot,
Cheyenne, Crow, and Pawnee

Northeast groups include:
Algonquian, Iroquois, Chippewa,
Mahican, Micmac, and Shawnee

Great Basin groups include:
Ute, Paiute, and Kawaiisu

California groups include:
Maidu, Hupa, and Monache

Southwest groups include:
Navajo, Apache, Pueblo, and Hopi

Southeast groups include:
Creek, Cherokee, Caddo, Apalachee,
Calusa, and Chickasaw

TALES OF THE GREAT HARE

According to the tales told by Algonquian-speaking people, the god Michabo was a son of the West Wind and a bringer of light. Mighty in word and deed, he took the form of the rabbit's cousin, the hare.

Michabo, the Great Hare, was swimming in the ocean. With his powerful hind legs, he was an excellent swimmer. He dived deep down to where the sea was darkest blue, with his long ears streaming out behind him.

He had never swum so deep before, and he decided to see if he could reach the very bottom. On he went, deeper and deeper, until his lungs seemed fit to burst. Then he touched the ocean floor.

In triumph he plucked up a single grain of sand and swam back to the surface, clutching it in his paw. He then placed the trophy of his successful dive on the ocean surface. There it turned from a single grain into a thousand grains, and from a thousand into a million . . . until it grew into an island, then a continent, then larger still.

But how big was the land? The Algonquian tell how one day a wolf cub found itself on the edge of the land and decided to trek across it. By the time the wolf was fully grown, the other side was still too far ahead to see . . . but on he went, determined to reach the edge. For years and years he wandered, until, finally, his years ran out–he had reached old age and still hadn't completed his journey. When the animal lay down to die after a long life, the end of the land was still nowhere in sight. *That's* how big the land was.

Many peoples–of many groups and many races–came to live on this land. This piece of land, created from a single grain of sand, is what we now think of as Earth, and Michabo, the Great Hare, was its creator.

One day Great Hare was walking past a mighty river, which flowed between the trees like a giant silver snake. A boy stood in the shallows of the crystal-clear water, as still as the stones on the rocky river bed. Suddenly there was a flash of silvery light beneath the surface as a fish darted by. The boy hurled a spear at it—the sharp point only narrowly missing its target. The boy picked up the spear and became still once more, to wait for the next fish to swim by.

Great Hare lay down against a rock in the afternoon sunshine and thought about what he had just seen. He knew that by the time the boy had grown into a young man, he would probably be a fine hunter and would catch many fish with his spear for his wife and children. But surely there was an easier way to catch food?

Still thinking about this problem, Great Hare drifted off to sleep in the lazy afternoon sun. When he awoke, he felt a tingling on the top of his head. Imagine his surprise when he found that while he'd been sleeping, a spider had spun her delicate web between his ears!

But Great Hare was not angry. He laughed. He carefully caught the spider between his paws and gently placed her on a rock, where she scuttled for cover . . . but not before he had studied the delicate web she'd spun. It had given the god an idea.

The spider used her web to catch flies . . . flies she would later eat. She would spin her web on a branch—or even between the ears of a god—and wait for the flies to fly into it and become trapped.

Why not make a similar web from twine? It would have to be much bigger and stronger than the spider's web, but the idea was the same. Instead of casting a web into the air to catch flies, people could cast a net into the water to catch fish. And that is how the fishing net was invented—thanks to Great Hare and a spider.

On another occasion Michabo, the Great Hare, had left his home in the East—the place of light and good—and was sitting by another riverbank, drawing patterns in the wet sand with a twig. A man and woman passed by, greeted him, then went into the forest to pick herbs.

Without much thought Great Hare lazily drew simple outline pictures of them.

On their return they passed the Great Hare once more, and the woman glanced down at the images he'd drawn in the sand. She asked him what he was doing.

"Drawing pictures," he told them.

The man laughed. "That looks like the two of us walking side by side," he said with glee and pointed at the pictures in the sand.

"And those trees look like the forest over there," said the woman excitedly. "You are clever! It's like a story–not in words but in squiggles in the sand. Anyone who sees them will know a man and woman went into the forest."

"And came back with herbs," said the Great Hare, drawing another picture in the row. He leapt up in delight and sniffed the wind with his twitching nose, just as any ordinary hare does when it has a great idea.

"If I were to draw several pictures, each with a different meaning, then people could use them to leave each other messages," he said gleefully. "They wouldn't even have to be in the same place at the same time to speak to each other. What a thoroughly useful invention!"

And that is how the Algonquian say that picture writing was invented.

Time and time again Michabo proved himself a true friend to the people. He taught them many tricks in hunting–such as when to wait and when to pounce and ways to track prey downwind so that it won't catch the hunter's scent in the air–and he gave them many lucky charms to help them. But before each winter came, he would leave his human friends behind and go home for his long sleep, ready to return the next spring.

Creator, inventor, or trickster, there was always a place in the Great Hare's heart for his people, and in the hearts of the Algonquian for him.

THE QUEST FOR HEALING

Nekumonta, the Iroquois brave, never killed an animal for sport and loved the plants and trees around him. When a terrible plague descended on his village, his kindness to nature was repaid.

Winter had come to Nekumonta's village, and the snow was thick on the ground. But something worse than snow had come to visit the village that year—a dreadful plague. No one seemed safe—men, women, and children had all died from it. Those who hadn't yet caught the plague were exhausted from looking after the ill and sending off the dead.

Never had there been such sadness in the village. Husbands lost wives. Mothers lost children. Brothers lost sisters. Whole families were wiped out. Along with the snow came the plague . . . and along with the plague came sadness and despair.

Nekumonta had lost all his family to this terrible disease—all, that is, except for his beautiful wife, Shanewis. But now she had caught the disease, and her days among the living were numbered. She called for Nekumonta and insisted that he carry her outside.

When he protested, she said, "Husband, we both know that death will come whether I stay in the warmth or sit beneath the sky, where I can hear the spirits of my dead loved ones call my name. Please, please, do as I ask."

So Nekumonta wrapped his beloved wife in extra blankets and carried her into the open, laying her down in a place cleared of snow. Sure enough the grey skies were filled with the spirits of those who had departed this life, and they called down to Shanewis.

"Join us," they cried out. "Be free from the pain and suffering brought by the plague."

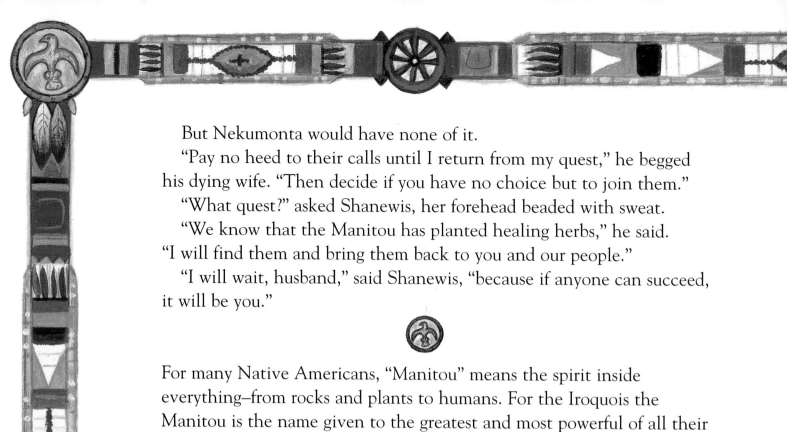

But Nekumonta would have none of it.

"Pay no heed to their calls until I return from my quest," he begged his dying wife. "Then decide if you have no choice but to join them."

"What quest?" asked Shanewis, her forehead beaded with sweat.

"We know that the Manitou has planted healing herbs," he said. "I will find them and bring them back to you and our people."

"I will wait, husband," said Shanewis, "because if anyone can succeed, it will be you."

For many Native Americans, "Manitou" means the spirit inside everything–from rocks and plants to humans. For the Iroquois the Manitou is the name given to the greatest and most powerful of all their gods. His healing herbs would cure Shanewis . . . if only her husband could find them.

With his wife back in the warmth of their home, Nekumonta set off on his quest for the healing herbs. This would have been a difficult task at the best of times, but it was made even harder by the snow, which covered much of the ground. Nekumonta had to dig in the snow to try to find the herbs, and he didn't even know where they were planted. Using his knowledge of nature, he could only guess at where they were likely to grow.

At the end of the day, a rabbit bounced past Nekumonta as he was kneeling in the snow, digging away with his hands.

"Do you know where the Manitou has planted the herbs that will help cure my people?" Nekumonta asked, but the rabbit didn't know and continued on its way, leaving behind its tracks in the snow.

Later, as darkness fell at the end of the short winter's day, the Iroquois brave caught sight of a grizzly bear watching him from the depths of the forest. Nekumonta asked the bear about the healing herbs, but the bear knew nothing, and lumbered off between the trees.

The next afternoon, having traveled far and wide, Nekumonta saw a doe–a female deer–chewing at the shoots of a plant sticking out of the snow. The doe recognized him, and knowing that he was a friend to the animals and meant her no harm, she did not run and hide.

Nekumonta patted her gently and said, "Everyone in my village is dying, and my beautiful wife, Shanewis, is among them. If you know where the Manitou has planted the healing herbs, please lead me to them. They are our only hope."

But the doe didn't know where the Manitou had planted the herbs, so she twitched her ears and disappeared into the forest. The story was the same with every animal he met after that. None of them could help him.

On the third night Nekumonta was near to giving up. Weak and exhausted, he wrapped himself in his blanket and fell asleep.

While he slept, the animals of the forest held a meeting.

"Nekumonta is a good human," said the grizzly bear. "He only kills when he has to, as is the way with us animals."

"And he treats our homes with respect, too," said the rabbit. "He cares about the trees and plants around him."

"Do you think we should help him?" asked the doe.

"Yes," said the rabbit. "But how can we?"

"Perhaps we could call to the great Manitou for his help?" suggested the grizzly bear. "Then he will realize that all living things want Nekumonta to succeed in his quest."

So the rabbit, the grizzly bear, the doe, and all the other animals stood in a clearing in the forest and cried out to the Manitou to save Shanewis from the plague. The Manitou heard their cries and, touched by the animals' loyalty to a human, decided to help Nekumonta.

That night Shanewis came to Nekumonta in a dream—pale-faced and very thin. She began to sing him a strange and beautiful song, but he could not understand the words, and they soon turned into the music of a waterfall.

When he awoke, the music of the waterfall was still there with its sparkling chorus of voices—as pure and crystal-clear as spring water.

It said, "Find us. . . . Free us. . . . Then Shanewis and your people shall be saved."

But despite the beautiful music, there was no waterfall–not even a tiny stream–to be seen.

"Who are you?" called Nekumonta.

"We are the Healing Waters," said the chorus. "Free us."

"Where are you?" cried Nekumonta in despair, for the chorus of sparkling voices sounded so near, yet he could not find it.

"Free us," sang the chorus once more.

With a new lease on life, Nekumonta hunted high and low, but he couldn't find the Healing Waters anywhere . . . even though the voice of the chorus remained strong. Then he realized why. The Healing Waters were flowing directly beneath his feet. They were an underground spring!

Watched by the animals of the forest, Nekumonta first scraped away the snow, then hacked away at the hard soil with a flint, until a jet of water spurted high into the air and began flowing down the hillside. He had found the Healing Waters!

Exhausted, Nekumonta stepped into the path of the ice-cold waters and bathed himself in them. Their magical powers gave him strength, and all his tiredness was suddenly gone. Now he felt fitter and stronger than he had ever felt before.

He filled a skin bottle with the Healing Waters and ran down the hillside to the village. The other villagers rushed out of their homes to greet him.

"We are saved!" he cried. "We are saved!"

Soon everyone from the village had drunk and bathed in the waters and were well again. They thanked Nekumonta with all their hearts. He had succeeded in his quest, and the plague had been defeated.

When Nekumonta learned of the part the animals had played in helping him to save Shanewis and the village, he gave them thanks. In turn the animals gave thanks to the great Manitou who is, after all, master of everything. Nekumonta and Shanewis lived for many summers and had many children.

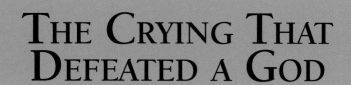

THE CRYING THAT DEFEATED A GOD

To the Algonquian-speaking people, Glooskap was a great god and trickster. He was afraid of no one and believed that there was nothing and nobody he could not conquer.

Glooskap had been away from his people for a long time. He had been away facing his enemies and had defeated them all through his bravery, cunning, and quick wit.

When he returned to one of his groups, Glooskap boasted about just how great he was. "There is no one left in this world who doesn't fear me or won't obey me," he said.

"Are you sure about that, master?" asked a woman. "I know of one who will not obey you."

Surprised at the news, but thrilled by the challenge, Glooskap demanded to know the name of this being.

"He is called Wasis," said the woman.

"And he does not fear me?" asked Glooskap.

"No," said the woman. "He always does exactly what he wants. He will not obey even you, master."

"Then this Wasis must be a very mighty one," said Glooskap.

"In his way," agreed the woman.

"Is he as tall as the Kewawkqu'?" Glooskap demanded. The Kewawkqu' were a race of giants and magicians.

"No," said the woman. "He is smaller than a goblin."

"Is his magic greater than the Medecolin?" Glooskap demanded. The Medecolin were cunning sorcerers.

"No," said the woman. "He knows no magic."

"Is he as wicked as Pamola?" Glooskap demanded. Pamola was an evil spirit of the night.

"No," said the woman. "Wasis is none of these things. He is not a giant. He is not a sorcerer, and there is no wickedness in him at all."

"Yet he does not fear me, and he will not obey me!" boomed Glooskap, who was most puzzled by the thought of the mighty Wasis. "Will you take me to him?"

"If you wish it, master," said the woman. "Wasis lives close by. Come."

With that she led Glooskap to an ordinary wigwam. The dome-shaped house was made from a wooden frame covered with pieces of birch bark sewn together.

"Wasis lives here in the village?" asked Glooskap, shocked at the very suggestion. Why had he never heard of him? And why didn't someone as mighty as he live in one of the grander wigwams, with animal skins instead of bark for walls?

"Yes," said the woman. "This is his home."

They entered the wigwam, and the god looked around. It seemed familiar. "Isn't this your home?" he asked.

The woman nodded her head. "Yes, master, but now it is Wasis' home, too."

"Where is he, then?" asked Glooskap.

The woman pointed to a baby who was sitting on a rug, sucking a piece of maple sugar. "That is Wasis," she said.

"But he is no more than a baby!" Glooskap said, laughing loudly.

"No more and no less, master," the woman agreed. "He is my son." She knew that Glooskap was always away having adventures and had never had to look after a child in his whole life. He didn't know how different young children are from other human beings!

Glooskap decided to use his charm to make Wasis obey him. He smiled at the baby. "Come here, Wasis," he said.

Wasis smiled back, but didn't move. He just sat in the middle of the rug, gurgling happily to himself.

Then Glooskap put his hands to his mouth and made the sound of bird song.

It was beautiful music, and Wasis' mother was enchanted by the sound. But it was not intended for her. It was intended to attract the attention of Wasis, and he wasn't in the least bit interested. He showed far more interest in the piece of maple sugar he was sucking.

Furious that anyone dared ignore him–a mighty god–Glooskap exploded in a terrible rage. "Come here at once!" he shouted at Wasis, but still this had no effect.

Upset by this stranger who had come into his home and was now shouting and waving his arms around, Wasis refused to obey the god. He burst into tears. The louder Glooskap's rage became, the louder Wasis howled . . . and still he would not move from his spot on the rug.

Finally Glooskap turned to magic. He began to sing a song so powerful that it was enough to wake the dead. Some say that it was a song so woven with magic that it made all the evil spirits scurry to the deepest depths of Mother Earth to escape from it.

Wasis stopped howling and seemed soothed by the tune. But soon he was bored by it–he yawned loudly, and his eyelids began to droop.

Utterly defeated, Glooskap fled the wigwam, shaking with anger. The woman scooped up Wasis in her arms and held him close to her. She walked out through the doorway and watched the enraged god stomping off through the camp. There would be no more boasts from him that day!

The baby sensed the familiar smell of his mother and felt the warmth of her body against his. He smiled and looked lovingly into her eyes. There was no more crying.

"I think the master Glooskap has learned an important lesson today, Wasis," she said.

"Goo!" said Wasis, and they both went back inside.

And that is how the greatest of gods was defeated by the smallest of children and why whenever a baby says "Goo!" it is to remind us of the time when Wasis put Glooskap firmly in his place.

BLACK BIRD, BRIGHT SKIES

Today the land of the Canadian Inuit has daylight for half the year and night for the other half. But, according to an Inuit myth, that wasn't always so. It used to be a place of eternal night.

Once, back in the mists of time, the home of the Inuit was a place of total darkness. It was a bleak place of frozen wastes, where the biting cold cut right through the furs worn by the Inuit and sank its teeth into the very marrow of their bones. But worse than the cold was the never-ending night. Midnight or midday, the sky was as black as the shapes of the seals swimming beneath the ice.

In this darkness babies were born, igloos were built, and animals were hunted. Time seemed meaningless, because there were no days to count. The people of this terrible wasteland had only their seal-oil lamps to lighten their darkness.

To pass the time, the Inuit spent much of their lives indoors telling each other stories, but one of the most popular storytellers wasn't a human at all. He was a crow.

Unlike the Inuit this bird had traveled far and wide. In one hour his wings could carry him farther than a man or woman could walk in a day on the treacherous ice with no sunlight to guide them. But, then again, hours and days meant nothing to the Canadian Inuit.

The crow told them of all the other lands he'd seen and of a thing called daylight.

"What is this daylight you speak of?" asked a young hunter. "I do not understand."

"It is brighter than the lightning that lights up the sky in a storm," said the crow. "But, unlike lightning, it isn't gone in a flash."

"You mean the sky stays bright?" said the young hunter.

"Yes," said the crow. "Instead of the sky being as dark as the pupils in the center of your eyes, it is as light as the white that surrounds them."

"How can this be possible?" asked an old woman. "I have lived longer than any of you sitting in this circle, and I have never seen this thing you call daylight."

"None of us has really seen *anything* clearly!" cried the young hunter. "We live in a world of shadows . . . a world lit by the yellow glow of our seal-oil lamps. Without that we would be completely blind."

"Then bring us some of this daylight, Crow, to help us in our daily lives," pleaded the old woman. "Not to prove the truth of what you say, for we do not doubt your word, but to help us," she said.

Crow was always eager to help the Inuit. He had no real reason to visit their land, but they were his friends, and that was why he always returned to them.

"Yes," added the young hunter. "Will you travel to the world of daylight and bring back a piece for us?"

"I'll try," said the crow.

The next morning–though no one could tell that it was morning, for the sky was still black–the crow set off on his journey. A crowd of people had gathered in the darkness to see him off. "Good luck," they cried, but the moment he took to the skies, they could no longer see their friend, for his feathers were as black as the sky through which he flew.

On he flew until he saw a glimmering of light on the horizon. At last he had reached the land of daylight, and then–and only then–did he settle down, completely exhausted, to sleep.

When the crow awoke, he thought of the task that lay ahead of him. The Inuit were good people. Because food was scarce in their land, they were always happy to share what little they had among them. Crow knew that this wasn't the way of all people. He knew that those who owned daylight would not willingly give him a piece as a gift, however small. He would have to steal it.

Crow flew to a village and looked for the house of the chief, because he knew that the most important person in the village would be in charge of daylight. He rested on the window ledge and saw a small boy crawling around on a bearskin rug, watched by his loving grandfather, the chief.

Crow could see from the chief's expression that he loved his grandson dearly and that he'd do anything for him. The boy could ask for anything and, to make him happy, his grandfather would give it to him—Crow had no doubt about that.

Some say that the crow turned himself into a speck of dust and crawled right inside the little boy's ear. Others say that Crow spoke to the boy once the chief had left his house to help his daughter carry in a sealskin bucket of water. Either way, Crow whispered to the boy: "Ask your grandfather for a piece of daylight . . . a small piece will do, with a length of string to hold it by."

So the excited boy cried, "Grandpa! Grandpa! Let me play with a small piece of daylight."

But daylight was far too precious to be played with, so the chief tried to distract his grandson. "Not now, child," he said. "Let me tell you the story of Nanook, the white bear."

He took down a tiny bear carved from the tusk of a walrus and put it on a rug next to the boy. Then he began to tell his grandson his favorite story—the Inuit tale of how a polar bear saved a man's life by warming him with his body and catching fish for him to eat, and how he taught the man that bears and humans were brothers.

But for once the story did not weave its magic. The boy could think of nothing but the daylight. It was a piece of daylight that he wanted to play with, and after he started crying, it was a piece of daylight he was given—with a length of string to dangle it from.

"Thank you, Grandpa," the boy smiled, holding up the glowing orb.

Before anyone knew what was happening, Crow flapped down from the roof where he had been hiding and snatched the length of string.

He then flew straight out of the door, which had just been opened by the boy's father, returning home from a hunt.

Up into the air Crow flew, dodging the stream of arrows that were fired up at him by the chief and his villagers. With him he carried the piece of daylight, glowing like an orange ball. On he flew, never daring to stop as he brought daylight to his friends, the Inuit.

It was only a small piece, of course, because Crow wouldn't have been able to carry anything much larger, but it was big enough to bring his friends light and warmth for half of every year. For the first time they had natural light to see by. The old woman, the young hunter, and all the other Inuit were very grateful for what the crow had done, risking his life to bring them daylight.

"Thank you," they said. "We shall never forget what you did for us. Your deeds will be told in stories by our children and their children. Your name will live on among our people forevermore."

In a land where hunting is still hard and food is still scarce, the Canadian Inuit never kill crows. They are friends of the birds, and now you know why.

THE CURSE OF
THE SNAKE'S MEAT

A Sioux chief and his braves were heading homeward across the plains. Tired and hungry, they were in search of food. The chief put his ear to the ground and could hear what seemed to be the thundering of hoofs. . . .

"Buffalo!" he announced. "Many buffalo." His braves were delighted. They waited–arrows at the ready–to pick off some of the animals as they passed. Soon the noise grew loud enough for all of them to hear, and the ground shuddered underfoot.

"There must be a whole herd of them!" said one of the braves with glee. "We'll return home with fine hides as well as full stomachs."

But their excitement soon turned to horror when they saw what was coming toward them. This was no herd of buffalo–it was a giant rattlesnake, taller than a tepee. What they thought was the sound of hoofs turned out to be the monstrous rattle at the tip of its tail!

Rooted to the spot with fear, the chief somehow managed to pull an arrow from his quiver and let it loose at this terrifying beast. His aim was true, and the snake was killed with this single, well-placed shot.

Soon they were all eating snake meat–all, that is, except for the youngest brave. . . .

That night the braves woke up in screaming terror, to find that they had no arms or legs and that their skin was turning into scales. Only the youngest brave remained human, as his friends turned into wriggling snakes before his very eyes! Saddened and shaken, he returned to the village and told his people what had happened.

In the summer the snakes came to visit their old village. They did no harm and slithered across their loved ones who recognized them and so did not fear them. When winter came, the snakes left, and the villagers discovered that the braves' horses and possessions had gone, too.

THE GIANT OF THE LOGGING CAMPS

According to European settler legends, the greatest lumberjack of them all—some say the very first lumberjack—was a giant man called Paul Bunyan.

Mrs. Bunyan knew there was something special about her son Paul as soon as he was born. "Our boy is going to be something big in this world," she told her husband proudly, but she probably hadn't guessed quite how big.

By the time he could walk, her son was bigger and stronger than most of the men in town. Townsfolk knew who Paul Bunyan was, and it wasn't long before they had their own tale to tell about him.

One morning the townsfolk were awakened by a huge "BANG" followed by the shattering of glass—and the sound had come from the Bunyan house. People leapt out of their beds, pulled on their breeches and boots, and dashed over to see if they could help.

"What happened?" called out one, as Paul's father walked out of his front door, the ground covered in broken glass. "Are you all right?"

"We're all fine, thank you, friends," Paul's father assured them. "It's just that young Paul has a slight cold, and one of his sneezes blew the glass out of all our windows." The bleary-eyed townsfolk laughed and went back home for breakfast.

By the time he was a young man, Paul Bunyan wasn't just big—he was huge! No one ever got to measure just how tall he was, because there was no tape measure long enough. Paul quickly outgrew his hometown and decided to become a lumberjack in the forests. The job of the lumberjacks was to cut down trees for wood, so that others could build new homes and the furniture for those homes.

Wood was used to make wagons to carry people and goods, and to make ties for the tracks that carried the mighty steam trains. It was

used to build churches, hotels, and jails and to make telegraph poles so that people could send messages to one another.

Working as a lumberjack in a logging camp was hard work–*hungry* work–for strong men, and the logging camp Paul Bunyan set up wasn't like any other. Behind it was a lake, but this was no ordinary lake. Instead of crystal-clear blue waters, this lake was filled with a thick green bubbling liquid. This was a pea-soup lake–hot and ready to serve, night or day.

And you should have seen the griddle on top of the stove that the lumberjacks used to cook their pancakes. In order to grease it, two cooks had to strap hams to their feet and skate around on them, sizzling in the heat–that's how big it was!

Paul Bunyan's logging camp was the biggest and best there ever was. He did so much business that the bookkeeper–who kept a record of all the wood they sold–used more than 20 barrels of ink a week.

"The money we spend on all that ink could be better spent on new axes or extra food for the men," said the bookkeeper. "Any ideas on how we could make a saving?" he asked Paul Bunyan one day.

"By not dotting your *i*'s and not crossing your *t*'s," said Paul.

So that's exactly what the bookkeeper did, and he managed to save six barrels of ink in just over two weeks!

Everything about Paul Bunyan was larger than life–even his pet, which was a great big ox and no ordinary ox at that. This was a giant of an ox, and what's more, it was bright blue. And what did Paul call this enormous beast with its sharp horns and huge muscles? Babe.

Babe used to have a whole barn to himself–because he was so big–but he even grew too big for that. One morning Paul found Babe wearing the barn on his back like a saddle. The ox had outgrown it in the night, and now it was stuck on top of him!

There are many tall tales about the adventures of Paul Bunyan and Babe, each more unbelievable than the last. Take the time Paul had trouble getting a batch of logs down a winding road to the river.

Logs are straight and corners are bent, and the two don't go well together. There was only one road down to the river, and this winding one was it. Once the logs were in the water, they would be carried down to the sawmill by the current . . . but Paul had to get them down the road first.

He came up with a plan, using his brains and Babe's brawn. He built the ox a harness and tied it to one end of the winding road. With the promise of sugar lumps, Babe pulled the road until all the kinks, corners, and winding parts were pulled out of it, and it was as straight as a rope in a tug-of-war match.

But it wasn't just straight roads Paul Bunyan left behind him. Some claim he even created the Grand Canyon . . . by mistake! The canyon is a gorge in the earth in Arizona that's about 280 miles long and more than a mile deep in places. The story goes that it was made by Paul Bunyan's enormous pickax as he dragged it behind him on the ground—and he didn't even know he was doing it.

It seems that Paul Bunyan really did help to shape North America—in more ways than one!

THE MAN WHO PLANTED TREES

For the early European settlers who traveled by wagon to the unknown West, apple trees provided shelter, food, and a taste of home. Legend has it that most of the trees were planted by John Chapman, remembered to this day as Johnny Appleseed.

Johnny Appleseed was happy where he was. He'd heard stories of the West—a wild place of endless plains, huge mountains, and thick pine forests—and could think of no good reason why he should leave the safety of his beloved Massachusetts apple farm.

Johnny's farm was acre after acre of orchard, with hundreds of apple trees that bore beautiful blossoms in the springtime and delicious apples in the summer. Johnny loved his farm.

Like those around him, Johnny Appleseed was a simple, God-fearing person. He worked six days a week and went to church on the seventh. He was happy with life and happy to be in a country where there was enough land to share.

He loved the people, the land, and the food. And the food he loved most of all was apple pie, made from the apples from his very own farm. That Johnny's favorite food was apple pie came as no surprise to anyone. What did come as a surprise was his announcement one day that he himself was heading west.

"But why are you leaving?" asked a friend when he heard the news.

"Because an angel asked me to," said Johnny. "He came right out from behind a bush and gave me a mission in life."

"You?" his friend said, smiling in surprise. "Why you of all people, Johnny? All you know about is apples!"

"Which is why I was chosen," said Johnny. "My mission is to walk west, planting apple seeds as I go."

And that's exactly what he did. He rode no horse or mule. He carried no gun—just a few supplies, his precious apple seeds, and a spade to dig and turn the soil over with—which is how he got the name Johnny Appleseed.

Johnny Appleseed planted more than just apple seeds on his incredible trek westward. He planted plenty of goodwill, too. He cared about animals as well as people. One time he spent a cold winter's night sleeping out in the snow rather than force a mother bear and her cubs out of a warm hollow log that would have made an ideal shelter for him.

Wherever he went, he was made welcome. By the time he was an old man, he'd planted apple trees right across the plains. Some say that if it wasn't for Johnny Appleseed, there wouldn't be the phrase "as American as apple pie"!

Then one day the angel appeared to Johnny a second time. "Your work here is done," he told the old man. "Come plant a few apple seeds in heaven."

So Johnny and the angel left the earth together, leaving behind a country filled with beautiful orchards full of tasty apples.

KING OF THE WILD FRONTIER

Davy Crockett was a real-life American hero,
who died in the Battle of the Alamo in 1836.
But there are some stories about this legendary
man that are a little hard to believe. . . .

One day Davy Crockett and his friend Mike were out hunting.
"I've found a new way to catch raccoons," Davy told Mike.

"How's that?" asked Mike, eager to learn a new trick.

"What's the first thing that happens when a raccoon hears you
coming?" asked Davy.

"He runs up a tree," said Mike.

"Then what does the little fellow do?" asked Davy.

"He watches you," said Mike.

"And while he's watching me, I grin right back at him," said Davy.

"And?" asked Mike.

"And," said Davy Crockett, "I'm so ugly that he falls right out of his
tree when he sees me!"

Mike roared with laughter. "Even you're not that ugly, Davy!" he said.

"Shh!" whispered Davy. "See that raccoon up there?"

Mike peered into the gloom. "I can't say I do," he replied.

"There," said Davy. "You can just see its eye peering out at us
through the pine needles at the top of that fir tree."

"If you say so," said Mike.

So Davy Crockett stood up and stared right into the raccoon's eye.
He gave it one of his ugliest grins . . . and the bark fell off the tree!

Mike dashed forward. "That was no raccoon's eye," he gasped. "That
was a knot in the wood. You grinned such an ugly grin that you
frightened the bark right off the tree!"

Just then a real raccoon ran into the clearing.

It froze in its tracks as it caught sight of the two hunters and peered up at Davy. "You're Mr. Crockett–the finest hunter these woods have ever known," it said.

"That's true," said Davy, proudly. "I killed 105 bears in under a year."

"Then it would be an honor to be shot by you, Mr. Crockett," said the creature. "Please fire away."

Davy was deeply moved. "After what you said, I'd sooner be shot myself than shoot you," he sniffed, a tear forming in his eye.

"Why thank you," said the raccoon, hurrying off into the wood. "It's not that I doubt your word," he called back, "but I think I'll be off before you change your mind." With a flash of his tail, he was gone.

Davy looked at Mike. Mike looked at Davy.

"Do you think we've just been tricked by an animal?" asked Mike.

Davy Crockett shrugged. "One thing's for sure," he said. "That was the cleverest raccoon I've ever met!"

He may have been outsmarted by a raccoon, but Davy Crockett was also a hero. When Halley's comet came speeding toward Earth in 1835, some say that he snatched it by its fiery tail and sent it spinning harmlessly into space.

Mama and the Hairy Man

There are a number of different African American folk tales about the Hairy Man in the forest. He wasn't so much a fierce monster as a troublesome one, but he could be tricked. . . .

When Wiley went out walking, he usually took his two dogs with him, because his mama was worried that the Hairy Man would get him. "He got your father and now he wants you!" she warned him.

One day Wiley was in the forest about to cut some wood, when a wild pig went squealing by. Before Wiley had a chance to stop them, both his dogs chased off after it . . . and who should appear in the clearing? Why, the Hairy Man, of course.

Even though Wiley had never laid eyes on him before, he had no doubt who it was. The Hairy Man was very tall, very hairy, and had great big teeth. He was the ugliest, hairiest, tallest man Wiley had ever seen, but–come to think of it–the Hairy Man wasn't really a man at all. He was a monster . . . and this monster was grinning straight at Wiley.

Wiley ran up the nearest tree. He knew that the Hairy Man couldn't follow him, because he'd seen his feet. The Hairy Man's feet were like cow's hoofs, and Wiley knew that cows can't climb trees!

"Come on down, Wiley," said the Hairy Man, "and I'll show you some powerful magic!"

But Wiley wasn't going to fall for that trick. "My mama knows all the magic I'll ever need," he said, which was true. Mama was a root doctor. She knew the magic of the old African ways. "If I come down there, all you'll do is put me in that big sack of yours," said Wiley, staying put.

So the Hairy Man grabbed Wiley's ax and began chopping away at the trunk of the tree. It wouldn't be long before the tree came tumbling down with Wiley in it.

"Wait, Hairy Man!" he called. "It's time for me to do some praying."

"If you must," said the Hairy Man, who didn't really understand these things. He stopped chopping.

Instead of praying Wiley called out "Hoooo–Eeeeee!" But because Hairy Man wouldn't recognize a Christian prayer if you shouted one into his ear, he didn't realize he'd been tricked . . . until Wiley's hounds came running toward him through the forest. The Hairy Man ran off between the trees.

The next time Wiley met the Hairy Man, his dogs were tied up back at home, but he remembered a new trick his mama had taught him.

"Good afternoon, Mister Hairy Man," he said politely. "Mama tells me that your magic is really strong. She says that you can turn yourself into any kind of animal."

"Your mama's right," said the Hairy Man. "I can turn myself into an alligator or a giraffe or a–"

"Oh," said Wiley, looking disappointed. "Mama says turning into those kinds of creatures is easy. I was thinking you'd try something really difficult like a possum."

"Difficult?" laughed the Hairy Man. "I can turn into a possum as easy as that!" and he turned himself into a possum.

Before the possum had time to know what was happening, Wiley had rolled him into his own sack and tied a knot in the top–just as his mama had told him to. But then the bag went flat, and an ant crawled out of a tiny hole in the top. Wiley was up the nearest tree in a flash.

"It was clever turning into an ant like that," said the boy, "but can you make things disappear?"

"Like what?" asked the Hairy Man.

"Like rope," said the boy.

"It's done," said the Hairy Man.

"You mean you've made all the rope for miles around disappear?" asked Wiley.

The Hairy Man nodded. "Including the rope that was tying up my dogs?" grinned Wiley, then shouted, "Hoooo-Eeeeee!"

Muttering to himself, the Hairy Man hurried off into the forest. Wiley hurried home to tell Mama what had happened.

Mama decided that it was time to get rid of this Hairy Man once and for all. She knew that if you could trick a monster like him three times, he'd have to leave you alone. That was the way of things. She made some careful preparations, then used her powers to summon the Hairy Man to her home.

"I've come for Wiley," said the Hairy Man. "If you don't let me have him, I'm going to make your hens stop laying, your cow's milk dry up, and your goat go lame. What do you say to that, Mama?"

"Are you saying that if I give you my baby, you'll leave the rest of us alone forever?" she asked.

The Hairy Man nodded his big, hairy head. "Yes," he said.

"You promise?" asked Mama. "Because you know there's no going back on your word."

"Promise," said the Hairy Man, jumping up and down excitedly.

"Then take my baby," said Mama. "He's asleep in his bed."

The Hairy Man ran over to the bed, pulled back the sheets, and snatched up the baby that was lying there.

But this wasn't Mama's baby boy, Wiley. This baby wasn't even human. What the Hairy Man held in his hands was a squealing pig.

"This isn't your baby!" cried the Hairy Man.

"Oh, yes it is, Hairy Man," said Mama. "I own his mother, the sow, and I owned him, too—only he's yours now!"

Wiley came out of hiding with his two dogs. "That's the third time we've tricked you, Hairy Man," he laughed. "So you'll have to leave us alone. We've won!"

Defeated, the Hairy Man went sulking back to the forest, where he's probably still muttering to himself to this day.

BRER RABBIT AND THE TAR BABY

The Brer Rabbit stories were first told by African American slaves and grew out of animal myths from the African homeland. "*Brer*" means "brother." These stories were first written down by a journalist for the Atlanta *Constitution* called Joel Chandler Harris.

"Rise and shine, Brer Fox!" said Brer Rabbit one bright morning, strolling past his sleepy-eyed enemy. Now Brer Fox was bigger than the rabbit, stronger than the rabbit, and had sharper teeth than the rabbit, but Brer Rabbit was always getting the better of him!

Brer Fox planned to change all that—forever. The reason why he looked so bleary-eyed and half asleep wasn't because that noisy Brer Rabbit had just waked him. No, the reason why Brer Fox was tired was because he'd been up to mischief in the moonlight.

He'd crept to the tar pit, where the black pitch bubbled out of the ground, and had shaped some tar to look like a baby rabbit.

Fox then took the tar baby and set it in the middle of the dirt track that he knew Brer Rabbit took to his lettuce patch every morning. Then he crept back home and curled up, pretending that he'd been asleep there all night.

When the rabbit reached the tar baby, he greeted it. "Good morning, youngster," he said. "Where's your mama and papa?"

Not surprisingly, the tar baby said nothing, because that's all it was: a baby made of tar. So Brer Rabbit gave it a shake—only to find that his paws stuck to it like glue. He then used his back legs to try to pull himself free from the sticky tar, and they got stuck, too.

Then Brer Fox popped up. He'd been hiding in a ditch, watching all the time. "It looks like I'll be having rabbit stew tonight!" he laughed.

"I think I'm going to cook you on the fire!" he said, grabbing Brer Rabbit by the ears.

"Oh, that's all right then," said the rabbit. "I thought you were going to throw me into the prickly patch of briars over there."

"On second thought, I'm going to skin you, then eat you," said the fox, annoyed that the rabbit didn't seem frightened by his threat.

"Just so long as you don't throw me into the briar patch," Brer Rabbit pleaded.

"Or I could hang you from a tree," said Brer Fox.

"Sounds nasty," agreed Brer Rabbit. "But not as nasty as the briar patch."

"Then it's into the briar patch you'll go!" cried the fox. Pulling the rabbit free of the tar baby, he threw him up in the air . . . and Brer Rabbit landed in the prickly briar patch.

"Thank you for letting me go, Brer Fox!" Brer Rabbit shouted. "You're forgetting that we rabbits were born and raised in the briar patch!" And, with that, he hopped away.

Once again Brer Rabbit had got the better of Brer Fox.

WHEN PEOPLE HAD WINGS

Myths of flying people, such as this one, were born out of slavery. Africans were kidnapped, brought to North America against their will, and forced to work as slaves, often for cruel masters. This myth is a story of hope and freedom.

John awoke with the sunrise. There was no breakfast for him, just more hard work in the cotton fields. His legs were sore from the driver's whip, and his belly ached with hunger. But still he worked all morning alongside the others, picking cotton under the hot sun.

Then the whispering started. There wasn't supposed to be any talking, and the overseer rode his horse between the cotton pickers, making sure that everyone was working hard. So the news–the joyous news–was whispered from person to person that Master Tom's slaves on the other side of the hill had sprouted wings and flown away.

"What do you mean flown?" whispered John to the old man who was doing the telling.

"What I say," said the man. "Didn't anyone ever tell you that back in Africa people can fly?"

"My papa's from Africa, but he can't fly," John protested, still picking cotton in case he caught the cruel eye of the overseer.

"That's because we lost the power when we were brought across the ocean," said the old man. "Our wings just shriveled up and died."

"It's true," whispered Mary. "I used to have wings–blacker than the blackbird's, glinting in the sun. But I lost them–the power and the wings." She suddenly looked sadder than she'd ever looked before, as she remembered long-lost days of soaring through the African skies.

"Then why do Master Tom's slaves still have the power?" whispered John. "And why didn't they fly away before now?"

But there the conversation stopped, because the driver strode past with his whip, glaring at each of them in turn.

When he had passed, the old man answered John. "Because the power was given back to them by the One Who Remembers–a seer with the gift to say the words that cause wings to grow," he said.

"Why didn't he share the words?" asked John. "Then someone from Master Tom's plantation could have told us!"

"Once the words are spoken and the magic has acted, they're forgotten by all except the one who spoke them," sighed Mary. "That is the way with some African magic."

John had a heavy heart. "If only the One Who Remembers was in our field," said John.

"But I am," said the old man, and he spoke the secret words.

Then he stood in the middle of the field and cried, "Join hands!" and all the slaves hurried forward and linked hands.

"Back to work!" cried the overseer, galloping toward them.

"Fly!" said the old man, and John felt his shirt tear as his newly grown wings ripped through the cloth, and he and everyone else in the circle took to the air.

They were flying! They were free!

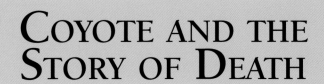

COYOTE AND THE STORY OF DEATH

Most Native North American groups tell tales of the fight between good and bad gods. Coyote appears as a bad god in the myths of many different groups. This is the story of how he brought death to humans, then regretted it.

When the world began, there was only water, or so the Maidu say. There was no land, no plants, no animals, and no people–just water, with the gods Kodoyanpe and Coyote floating on the surface. The gods decided to create the land and everything on it. Then they created people . . . but over time there were too many of them.

Kodoyanpe turned to Coyote. "What shall we do?" he asked. "There are too many people to fit on the earth we have created. Soon they'll run out of space."

"We could stop them from having any more children," Coyote suggested. He didn't care for humans in the way that Kodoyanpe did.

"No, that would be wrong," said Kodoyanpe. "Children bring joy and happiness to the people and hope for the future."

"What about death?" suggested Coyote.

"You mean that humans should die in the same way that plants and animals die?" asked Kodoyanpe. "It seems very cruel."

"It would solve the problem of there being too many of them," Coyote said. He really didn't care.

"But that would make everyone so unhappy," Kodoyanpe protested. "They would miss their loved ones terribly."

"They'd get used to it," snapped Coyote. Because Kodoyanpe seemed so concerned about these people, Coyote was beginning to enjoy having the opposite view. He didn't like it that Kodoyanpe always seemed to get his own way.

"I have an idea," said Kodoyanpe. "What if they were to come back to life after a while and change places with the next group whose turn it was to die?" He smiled broadly.

"No," said Coyote. "Death should be the end for people. There should be no going back."

Now, according to a tale the Caddo people tell—a group that lives far, far away from the Maidu—Coyote was overruled. It was decided that when people die, they should stay in a special house built by the chief shaman, until it was time to come back to life and return to their people and family. So when the time was right, the first person—a man—died, and his spirit was whisked away on a whirlwind to the shaman's house.

But Coyote would have none of it. Under the cover of darkness, he turned himself into the form of a vicious wild dog, like those we now call coyotes after him. He slunk into the doorway of the house for the resting dead and waited.

When the dead man's spirit reached the house, it found the entrance blocked by this frightening beast and dared not enter. So instead of resting a while and then returning to life, the dead man's spirit was condemned to search the skies for the path to the land of the spirits. When, at last, it found its way and entered that land, there was no way back . . . and that's how it has been for everyone since.

But according to the Maidu people, Coyote had his way much more easily. He argued and argued with Kodoyanpe until his brother god finally gave in and accepted the suggestion that humans should not come back to life. Either way, in both stories Coyote won, and death really did mean the end of life for humans.

Kodoyanpe and Coyote went to live among the humans. Kodoyanpe had always loved the people he'd created, and Coyote had never understood that love—until he had a son of his own. Coyote loved that little boy more than he could have imagined possible, so he was

overcome with grief when the boy was bitten by a snake.

"I'm dying, father," said the boy. "I can feel the poison in my veins. Help me."

Coyote snatched up the boy and hurried with him to see the chief shaman. "You must help him," cried Coyote. "He has been bitten by a snake."

The shaman looked at him sadly. "You are a god, and you can do nothing, mighty Coyote!" he said. "How do you expect me—a mere human—to do what you cannot?"

"But you must try," said Coyote, thrusting his son into the shaman's arms. "You are a medicine man."

The shaman looked down at the still body of the boy. "I'm sorry, Coyote," said the shaman. "There is nothing any of us can do now. Your child is already on his way to the land of the spirits."

Coyote threw back his head and howled with rage like a wild dog. "Will no one save my son?" he wailed. Then he went off in search of Kodoyanpe and when he found him, pleaded with him. "Kodoyanpe, I was wrong!" he said. "Death shouldn't be the end. Help me bring my son back to life. I cannot bear to be parted from him."

Kodoyanpe looked at Coyote and the lifeless boy in his arms. It saddened him that he could do nothing to help, but death meant death and that was of Coyote's own making.

"I'm sorry," said Kodoyanpe, and he truly was, for he hated to see anyone suffer such grief. "But what's done is done. We cannot undo it. Death is forever."

Coyote howled once more. "*Cannot* undo it, or *will not* undo it?" he howled.

His voice became a terrible snarl, and his shape changed until he became a wild dog once more.

"Grieve for your son, but do not be angry," urged Kodoyanpe. "Remember, it was you who wanted death to be the end!"

With his son dead and haunted by guilt and anger, Coyote roamed

the earth in his new form, making mischief wherever he went.

In time Kodoyanpe lost patience and warned the people against his brother god, Coyote.

"Kill him if you find him," he ordered. "For though the thought of killing him saddens me greatly, as long as Coyote is in the world, we will never be free from evil."

After many adventures a group of people chased Coyote onto a tiny island, where no food grew, and surrounded it in their canoes.

"We've trapped him!" said one.

"There's no escaping now," said another. "We'll starve him out, so he'll either die of hunger—"

"Or we'll kill him when he tries to escape," said the first. "Either way, that'll be an end to all that is bad in the world."

But Coyote was too clever for them. As evening came, he turned himself into a mist and drifted off the island on the breeze. Once clear of them he let out a great howl of victory, and the people knew that he had escaped from them.

Seeing the people close to despair, Kodoyanpe told them to build a giant canoe—big enough for everyone to fit inside. With everyone on board, Kodoyanpe then flooded the earth, in the hope of drowning Coyote . . . but Coyote had disguised himself and slipped on board with the others.

As the vast canoe drifted past the peak of a mountain—the only piece of earth not covered by the flood—Coyote leapt onto the mountain, which is how the Maidu people came to call it Canoe Mountain.

"This piece of land belongs to me now," Coyote declared, turning back into the form of a wild dog.

Kodoyanpe had to admit defeat. There was no way that he could ever rid the world of his cunning brother. This is why Coyote is still out there somewhere, and why we still have evil in the world today.

MYTHS AND LEGENDS RESOURCES

Here is just a sampling of other resources to look for. These resources on myths and legends are broken down into groups. Enjoy!

GENERAL MYTHOLOGY

The Children's Dictionary of Mythology *edited by David Leeming* (Franklin Watts, 1999). This volume is a dictionary of terms, names, and places in the mythology of various cultures around the world.

Creation Read-aloud Stories from Many Lands *retold by Ann Pilling* (Candlewick Press, 1997). This is a collection of sixteen stories retold in an easy style and presented in three general groups: beginnings, warmth and light, and animals.

The Crystal Pool: Myths and Legends of the World *by Geraldine McCaughrean* (Margaret K. McElderry Books, 1998). Twenty-eight myths and legends from around the world comprise this book. They include the Chinese legend "The Alchemist" and the Celtic legend "Culloch and the Big Pig."

Encyclopedia Mythica
http://www.pantheon.org/areas/mythology/
From this page of the *Encyclopedia Mythica* site you can select from any of five countries to have the mythology of that area displayed.

A Family Treasury of Myths from Around the World *retold by Viviane Koenig* (Abrams, 1998). This collection of ten stories includes myths from Egypt, Africa, Greece, and other places around the world.

Goddesses, Heroes and Shamans: The Young People's Guide to World Mythology *edited by Cynthia O'Neill and others* (Kingfisher, 1994). This book introduces the reader to over five hundred mythological characters from around the world.

Gods, Goddesses and Monsters: An Encyclopedia of World Mythology *retold by Sheila Keenan* (Scholastic, 2000). This beautifully illustrated book discusses the characters and themes of the myths of peoples from Asia to Africa, to North and South America.

The Golden Hoard: Myths and Legends of the World *retold by Geraldine McCaughrean* (Margaret K. McElderry Books, 1995). This book contains twenty-two myths and legends that are exciting, adventurous, magical, and poetic.

The Illustrated Book of Myths: Tales and Legends of the World *retold by Neil Philips* (Dorling Kindersley, 1995). This beautifully illustrated collection brings together many of the most popular of the Greek and Roman, Norse, Celtic, Egyptian, Native American, African, and Indian myths.

Kids Zone: Myths and Fables from Around the World
http://www.afroam.org/children/myths/myths.html
Just click on your choice of the sixteen stories listed, and it will appear in full text.

Legends http://www.planetozkids.com/oban/legends.htm
From this Web page you can get the full text of any of the many listings.

Mythical Birds and Beasts from Many Lands *retold by Margaret Mayo* (Dutton, 1996). This book is a collection of stories that illustrate the special powers of birds and beasts that have become a part of folklore around the world.

Mythology *by Neil Philip* (Alfred A. Knopf, 1999). This superbly illustrated volume from the "Eyewitness Books" series surveys the treatment of such topics as gods and goddesses, the heavens, creation, the elements, and evil as expressed in various mythologies around the world.

Mythology *CD-ROM for Mac and Windows* (Thomas S. Klise, 1996). Educational games and puzzles, a glossary, and a testing section are all part of this CD introduction to Greek and Roman mythology.

Myths and Legends *by Neil Philip* (DK Publishing, 1999). More than fifty myths and legends from around the world are explained through works of art, text, and annotation by one of the world's foremost experts on mythology and folklore.

The New York Public Library Amazing Mythology: A Book of Answers for Kids *by Brendan January* (John Wiley, 2000). Over two hundred questions and answers introduce myths from many ancient cultures, including Egyptian, Greek, Roman, Celtic, Norse, and Native American.

Plays from Mythology: Grades 4-6 *by L.E. McCullough* (Smith and Kraus, 1998). Twelve original plays are included, each with suggestions for staging and costumes.

Sources for Mythology
http://www.best.com/~atta/mythsrcs.html
In addition to defining mythology and distinguishing it from legend and folklore, this Web site lists primary sources for myths from many regions of the world, as well as magazines, dictionaries, and other resources relating to mythology.

Sun, Moon and Stars *retold by Mary Hoffman* (Dutton, 1998). More than twenty myths and legends from around the world, all explaining what was seen in the sky, make up this exquisitely illustrated book.

AFRICAN

African Gods and their Associates
http://www3.sympatico.ca/untangle/africang.html
This Web page gives you a list of the African gods with links to further information about them.

African Myths
http://www.cybercomm.net/~grandpa/africanmyths.html
Full text of several tales from the Kenya, Hausa, Ashanti, and Nyanja tribes are included in this Web site.

Anansi and the Talking Melon *retold by Eric A. Kimmel* (Holiday House, 1994). Anansi, a legendary character from Africa, tricks Elephant and some other animals into thinking that the melon in which he is hiding can talk.

Children's Stories from Africa *4 Video recordings (VHS)* (Monterey Home Video, 1997). Among the African Legends on this page: "How the Hare Got His Long Legs," "How the Porcupine Got His Quills," "The Brave Sititunga," and "The Greedy Spider."

The Hero with an African Face: Mythic Wisdom of Traditional Africa *by Clyde W. Ford* (Bantam, 2000). "The Hero with an African Face" is only one of the several stories included in this book, which also includes a map of the peoples and myths of Africa and a pronunciation guide for African words.

Kings, Gods and Spirits from African Mythology
retold by Jan Knappert (Peter Bedrick Books, 1993). This illustrated collection contains myths and legends of the peoples of Africa.

Legends of Africa *by Mwizenge Tembo* (Metro Books, 1996). This indexed and illustrated volume is from the "Myths of the World" series.

Myths and Legends *retold by O. B. Duane* (Brockhampton Press, 1998). Duane has vividly retold some of the most gripping African tales.

CELTIC

Celtic Myths *retold by Sam McBratney* (Peter Bedrick, 1997). This collection of fifteen illustrated stories draws from English, Irish, Scottish, and Welsh folklore.

Excalibur *retold by Hudson Talbott* (Books of Wonder, 1996). In this illustrated story from the legends of King Arthur, Arthur receives his magical sword, Excalibur

Irish Fairy Tales and Legends *retold by Una Leavy* (Robert Rinehart, 1996). Cuchulainn, Deirdre, and Fionn Mac Cumhail are only three of the legendary characters you will meet in this volume.

Irish Myths and Legends
http://www.mc.maricopa.edu/users/shoemaker/
   Celtic/index.html
This Web site is for those more serious in their study of Irish myths and legends.

King Arthur *by Rosalind Kerven* (DK Publishing, 1998). This book from the "Eyewitness Classic" series is a retelling of the boy who was fated to be the "Once and Future King" It includes illustrated notes to explain the historical background of the story.

Robin Hood and His Merry Men *retold by Jane Louise Curry* (Margaret K. McElderry, 1994). This collection contains seven short stories of the legendary hero Robin Hood, who lived with his band of followers in Sherwood Forest.

The World of King Arthur and his Court: People, Places, Legend and Love *by Kevin Crossley-Holland* (Dutton, 1998). The author combines legend, anecdote, fact, and speculation to help answer some of the questions regarding King Arthur and his chivalrous world.

CHINESE

Asian Mythology *by Rachel Storm* (Lorenz, 2000). Included in this volume are myths and legends of China.

Chinese Culture
http://chineseculture.about.com/culture/
   chineseculture/msub82.htm
Use this Web page as a starting point for further exploration about Chinese myths and legends.

Chinese Mythology by *Anne Birrell* (Johns Hopkins, 1999). This comprehensive introduction to Chinese mythology will meet the needs of the more serious and the general reader

Chinese Myths and Legends *retold by O. B. Duane and others* (Brockhampton Press, 1998). Introductory notes by the author give further explanation of the thirty-eight stories included in this illustrated volume.

Dragons and Demons by *Stewart Ross* (Cooper Beech, 1998). Included in this collection of myths and legends from Asia are the Chinese myths "Chang Lung the Dragon" and "The Ugly Scholar."

Dragons, Gods and Spirits from Chinese Mythology *retold by Tao Tao Liu Sanders* (Peter Bedrick Books, 1994). The stories in this book include ancient myths about nature, the gods, and creation as well as religious legends.

Fa Mulan: The Story of a Woman Warrior *retold by Robert D. San Souci* (Hyperion, 1998). Artists Jean and Mou-Sien Tseng illustrate this Chinese legend of a young heroine who is courageous, selfless, and wise.

Land of the Dragon: Chinese Myth by *Tony Allan* (Time-Life, 1999). This volume from the "Myth and Mankind" series includes many of China's myths as well as examination of the myth and its historical roots.

Selected Chinese Myths and Fantasies
http://www.chinavista.com/experience/story/story.html
From this Web site and its links you will find several Chinese myths that are enjoyed by children as well as the history of Chinese mythology.

EGYPTIAN

Egyptian Gods and Goddesses by *Henry Barker* (Grosset and Dunlap, 1999). In this book designed for the young reader, religious beliefs of ancient Egypt are discussed, as well as their gods and goddesses.

Egyptian Mythology A-Z: A Young Reader's Companion by *Pat Remler* (Facts on File, 2000). Alphabetically arranged, this resource defines words relating to Egyptian mythology.

Egyptian Myths *retold by Jacqueline Morley* (Peter Bedrick Books, 1999). Legends of the pharaohs, myths about creation, and the search for the secret of all knowledge, make up this illustrated book.

The Gods and Goddesses of Ancient Egypt by *Leonard Everett Fisher* (Holiday House, 1997). This artist/writer describes thirteen of the most important Egyptian gods.

Gods and Myths of Ancient Egypt by *Mary Barnett* (Regency House, 1996). Beautiful color photographs are used to further explain the text in this summary of Egyptian mythology.

Gods and Pharaohs from Egyptian Mythology *retold by Geraldine Harris* (Peter Bedrick Books, 1992). The author gives some background information about the Ancient Egyptians and then retells more than twenty of their myths.

Myth Man's Egyptian Homework Help
http://egyptmyth.com/
Cool Facts and Fun for Kids and *Egyptian Myth* Encyclopedia are only two of the many wonderful links this page will lead you to.

Myths and Civilizations of the Ancient Egyptians by *Sarah Quie* (Peter Bedrick Books, 1998). The author intersperses Egypt's myths with a history of its civilization in this illustrated volume.

The Secret Name of Ra *retold by Anne Rowe* (Rigby Interactive Library, 1996). In this Egyptian myth, Isis tricks Ra into revealing his secret name so that she and her husband Osiris can become rulers of the earth.

Tales from Ancient Egypt *retold by George Hart* (Hoopoe Books, 1994). The seven tales in this collection include stories of animals, of Isis and Horus, of a sailor lost on a magic island, and of pharaohs and their magicians.

Who's Who in Egyptian Mythology by *Anthony S. Mercatante* (Scarecrow Press, 1995). The author has compiled a concise, easy-to-use dictionary of ancient Egyptian deities.

GREEK

Allta and the Queen: A Tale of Ancient Greece by *Priscilla Galloway* (Annick Press, 1995). This made-up story, which is based on Homer's epic poem, *The Odyssey*, reads like a novel.

Cupid and Psyche *retold by M. Charlotte Craft* (Morrow Junior Books, 1996). This classic love story from Greek mythology will appeal to young and old.

Gods and Goddesses by *John Malam* (Peter Bedrick Books, 1999). This volume is packed with information about the important gods and goddesses of ancient Greece, including Zeus, Hera, Athena, and Hades.

Greek and Roman Mythology by *Dan Nardo* (Lucent, 1998). The author examines the historical development of Greco-Roman mythology, its heroes, and its influence on the history of Western civilization.

Guide for Using D'Aulaires' Book of Greek Myths in the Classroom by *Cynthia Ross* (Teacher Created Materials, 1993). This reproducible book includes sample plans, author information, vocabulary-building ideas, cross-curricular activities, quizzes, and many ideas for extending this classic work.

Hercules by *Robert Burleigh* (Harcourt Brace, 1999). Watercolor and color pencil illustrations help to tell the story of Hercules's final labor in which he went back to the underworld and brought back the three-headed dog, Cerberus.

Medusa by *Deborah Nourse Lattimire* (Joanna Cotler Books, 2000). The author/illustrator of this book re-creates the tragedy of one of the best-known Greek myths, the tale of the beautiful Medussa whose conceit causes a curse be placed on her.

The Myths and Legends of Ancient Greece *CD-ROM for Mac and Windows* (Clearvue, 1996). This CD conveys the heroic ideals and spirit of Greek mythology as it follows ten of the best-known myths.

Mythweb http://www.mythweb.com/
This Web page provides links to Greek gods, heroes, an encyclopedia of mythology, and teacher resources.

Pegasus, the Flying Horse *retold by Jane Yolen* (Dutton, 1998). This Greek myth tells of how Bellerophon, with the help of Athena, tames the winged horse Pegasus and conquers the monstrous Chimaera.

The Race of the Golden Apples *retold by Claire Martin* (Dial, 1991). Caldecott Medal winners Leo and Diane Dillon have illustrated this myth of Atalanta, the beautiful Greek princess.

The Random House Book of Greek Myths by *Joan D. Vinge* (Random House, 1999). The author retells some of the famous Greek myths about gods, goddesses, humans, heroes, and monsters, explaining the background of the tales and why these tales have survived.

The Robber Baby: Stories from the Greek Myths *retold by Anne Rockwell* (Greenwillow Books, 1994). Anne Rockwell, a well-known name in children's literature, has put together a superbly retold collection of myths that will be enjoyed by readers of all ages.

NORSE

Beowulf by *Welwyn Wilton Katz* (Groundwood, 2000). The illustrations in this classic legend are based on the art of the Vikings.

Favorite Norse Myths *retold by Mary Pope Osborne* (Scholastic, 1996). These fourteen tales of Norse gods, goddesses, and giants are based on the oldest written sources of Norse mythology, *Prose Edda* and *Poetic Edda*.

The Giant King by *Rosalind Kerven* (NTC Publishing Group, 1998). Photos of artifacts from the Viking Age illustrate these two stories that are rooted in Norse mythology.

Gods and Heroes from Viking Mythology by *Brian Branston* (Peter Bedrick Books, 1994). This illustrated volume tells the stories of Thor, Balder, King Gylfi, and other Nordic gods and goddesses

Handbook of Norse Mythology by *John Lindow* (Ambcc, 2001). For the advanced reader, this handbook covers the tales, their literary and oral sources, includes an A-to-Z of the key mythological figures, concepts and events, and so much more.

Kids Domain Fact File
http://www.kidsdomain.co.uk/teachers/resources/
 fact_file_viking_gods_and_goddesses.html
This child-centered Web page is a dictionary of Viking gods and goddesses.

Myths and Civilization of the Vikings by *Hazel Martell* (Peter Bedrick, 1998). Each of the nine stories in this book is followed by a non-fiction spread with information about Viking society.

Norse Mythology: The Myths and Legends of the Nordic Gods *retold by Arthur Cotterell* (Lorenz Books, 2000). This encyclopedia of the Nordic peoples' myths and legends is generously illustrated with fine art paintings of the classic stories.

Odins' Family: Myths of the Vikings *retold by Neil Philip* (Orchard Books, 1996). This collection of stories of Odin, the All-father, and the other Viking gods Thor, Tyr, Frigg, and Loer is full of excitement that encompasses both tragedy and comedy.

Stolen Thunder: A Norse Myth *retold by Shirley Climo* (Houghton Mifflin, 1994). This story, beautifully illustrated by Alexander Koshkin, retells the Norse myth about the god of Thunder and the recovery of his magic hammer Mjolnir, from the Frost Giany, Thrym.

NORTH AMERICAN

Buffalo Dance: A Blackfoot Legend *retold by Nancy Can Laan* (Little, Brown and Company, 1993). This illustrated version of the Native North American legend tells of the ritual performed before the buffalo hunt.

The Favorite Uncle Remus *by Joel Chandler Harris* (Houghton Mifflin, 1948). This classic work of literature is a collection of stories about Brer Rabbit, Brer Fox, Brer Tarrypin, and others that were told to the author as he grew up in the South.

Iktomi Loses his Eyes: A Plains Indian Story *retold by Paul Goble* (Orchard Books, 1999). The legendary character Iktomi finds himself in a predicament after losing his eyes when he misuses a magical trick.

The Legend of John Henry *retold by Terry Small* (Doubleday, 1994). This African American legendary character, a steel driver on the railroad, pits his strength and speed against the new steam engine hammer that is putting men out of jobs.

The Legend of the White Buffalo Woman *retold by Paul Goble* (National Geographic Society, 1998). This Native American Plains legend tells the story of the White Buffalo Woman who gave her people the Sacred Calf Pipe so that people would pray and commune with the Great Spirit.

Myths and Legends for American Indian Youth http://www.kstrom.net/isk/stories/myths.html Stories from Native Americans across the United States are included in these pages.

Snail Girl Brings Water: a Navajo Story *retold by Geri Keams* (Rising Moon, 1998). This retelling of a traditional Navajo re-creation myth explains how water came to earth.

The Woman Who Fell from the Sky: The Iroquois Story of Creation *retold by John Bierhirst* (William Morrow, 1993). This myth describes how the creation of the world was begun by a woman who fell down to earth from the sky country, and how it was finished by her two sons.

SOUTH AMERICAN (INCLUDING CENTRAL AMERICAN)

Gods and Goddesses of the Ancient Maya *by Leonard Everett Fisher* (Holiday House, 1999). With text and illustration inspired by the art, glyphs, and sculpture of the ancient Maya, this artist and author describes twelve of the most important Maya gods.

How Music Came to the World: An Ancient Mexican Myth *retold by Hal Ober* (Houghton Mifflin, 1994). This illustrated book, which includes author notes and a pronunciation guide, is an Aztec pourquoi story that explains how music came to the world.

Llama and the Great Flood *retold by Ellen Alexander* (Thomas Y. Crowell, 1989). In this illustrated retelling of the Peruvian myth about the Great Flood, a llama warns his master of the coming destruction and leads him and his family to refuge on a high peak in the Andes.

The Legend of the Poinsettia *retold by Tomie dePaola* (G. P. Putnam's Sons,1994). This beautifully illustrated Mexican legend tells of how the poinsettia came to be when a young girl offered her gift to the Christ child.

Lost Realms of Gold: South American Myth *edited by Tony Allan* (Time-Life Books, 2000). This volume, which captures the South American mythmakers' fascination with magic, includes the tale of the first Inca who built the city of Cuzco, as well as the story of the sky people who discovered the rain forest.

People of Corn: A Mayan Story *retold by Mary-Joan Gerson* (Little, Brown, 1995). In this richly illustrated creation story, the gods first try and fail, then try and fail again before they finally succeed.

Tales from the Rain Forest: Myths and Legends from the Amazonian Indians of Brazil *retold by Mercedes Dorson* (Ecco Press, 1997). Ten stories from this region include "The Origin of Rain" and "How the Stars Came to Be."

WHO'S WHO IN MYTHS AND LEGENDS

This is a cumulative listing of some important characters found in all eight volumes of the *World Book Myths and Legends* series.

A

Aegir (EE jihr), also called Hler, was the god of the sea and the husband of Ran in Norse myths. He was lord of the undersea world where drowned sailors spent their days.

Amma (ahm mah) was the creator of the world in the myths of the Dogon people of Africa. Mother Earth was his wife, and Water and Light were his children. Amma also created the people of the world.

Amun (AH muhn), later Amun-Ra, became the king of gods in later Egyptian myths. Still later he was seen as another form of Ra.

Anubis (uh NOO bihs) in ancient Egypt was the god of the dead and helper to Osiris. He had the head of a jackal.

Ao (ow) was a giant turtle in a Chinese myth. He saved the life of Kui.

Aphrodite (af ruh DY tee) in ancient Greece was the goddess of love. She was known for her beauty. The Romans called her Venus.

Arianrod (air YAN rohd) in Welsh legends was the mother of the hero Llew.

Arthur (AHR thur) in ancient Britain was the king of the Britons. He probably was a real person who ruled long before the age of knights in armor. His queen was Guinevere.

Athena (uh THEE nuh) in ancient Greece was the goddess of war. The Romans called her Minerva.

Atum (AH tuhm) was the creator god of ancient Egypt and the father of Shu and Tefnut. He later became Ra-Atum.

B

Babe (bayb) in North American myths was the big blue ox owned by Paul Bunyan.

Balder (BAWL dur) was the god of light in Norse myths. He was the most handsome of all gods and was Frigga's favorite son.

Balor (BAL awr) was an ancient chieftain in Celtic myths who had an evil eye. He fought Lug, the High King of Ireland.

Ban Hu (bahn hoo) was the dog god in a myth that tells how the Year of the Dog in the Chinese calendar got its name.

Bastet (BAS teht), sometimes Bast (bast) in ancient Egypt was the mother goddess. She was often shown as a cat. Bastet was the daughter of Ra and the sister of Hathor and Sekhmet.

Bellerophon (buh LEHR uh fahn) in ancient Greek myths was a hero who captured and rode the winged horse, Pegasus.

Blodeuwedd was the wife of Llew in Welsh legends. She was made of flowers woven together by magic.

Botoque (boh toh kay) in Kayapó myths was the boy who first ate cooked meat and told people about fire.

Brer Rabbit (brair RAB iht) was a clever trickster rabbit in North American myths.

C

Chameleon (kuh MEEL yuhn) in a Yoruba myth of Africa was a messenger sent to trick the god Olokun and teach him a lesson.

Conchobar (KAHN koh bahr), also called Conor, was the king of Ulster. He was a villain in many Irish myths.

Coyote (ky OH tee) was an evil god in myths of the Maidu and some other Native American people.

Crow (kroh) in Inuit myths was the wise bird who brought daylight to the Inuit people.

Cuchulain (koo KUHL ihn), also Cuchullain or Cuchulan, in Irish myths was Ireland's greatest warrior of all time. He was the son of Lug and Dechtire.

Culan (KOO luhn) in Irish myths was a blacksmith. His hound was killed by Setanta, who later became Cuchulain.

D

Davy Crockett (DAY vee KRAHK iht) was a real person. He is remembered as an American frontier hero who died in battle and also in legends as a great hunter and woodsman.

Dechtire (DEHK teer) in Irish myths was the sister of King Conchobar and mother of Cuchulain.

Deirdre (DAIR dray) in Irish myths was the daughter of Fedlimid. She refused to wed Conchobar. It was said that she would lead to Ireland's ruin.

Di Jun (dee joon) was god of the Eastern Sky in Chinese myths. He lived in a giant mulberry tree.

Di Zang Wang (dee zahng wahng) in Chinese myths was a Buddhist monk who was given that name when he became the lord of the underworld. His helper was Yan Wang, god of the dead.

Dionysus (dy uh NY suhs) was the god of wine in ancient Greek myths. He carried a staff wrapped in vines.

Dolapo was the wife of Kigbo in a Yoruba myth of Africa.

E

Eight Immortals (ihm MAWR tuhlz) in Chinese myths were eight ordinary human beings whose good deeds led them to truth and enlightenment. The Eight Immortals were godlike heroes. They had special powers to help people.

El Niño (ehl NEEN yoh) in Inca myths was the ruler of the wind, the weather, and the ocean and its creatures.

Emer (AYV ur) in Irish myths was the daughter of Forgal the Wily and wife of Cuchulain.

F

Fafnir (FAHV nihr) in Norse myths was a son of Hreidmar. He killed his father for his treasure, sent his brother Regin away, and turned himself into a dragon.

Frey (fray), also called Freyr, was the god of summer in Norse myths. His chariot was pulled by a huge wild boar.

Freya (FRAY uh) was the goddess of beauty and love in Norse myths. Her chariot was pulled by two large cats.

Frigga (FRIHG uh), also called Frigg, in Norse myths was the wife of Odin and mother of many gods. She was the most powerful goddess in Asgard.

Frog was an animal prince in an Alur myth of Africa. He and his brother, Lizard, competed for the right to inherit the throne of their father.

Fu Xi (foo shee) in a Chinese myth was a boy who, with his sister Nü Wa, freed the Thunder God and was rewarded. His name means Gourd Boy.

G

Gaunab was Death, who took on a human form in a Khoi myth of Africa. Tsui'goab fought with Gaunab to save his people.

Geb (gehb) in ancient Egypt was the Earth itself. All plants and trees grew from his back. He was the brother and husband of Nut and the father of the gods Osiris, Isis, Seth, and Nephthys.

Glooscap (glohs kap) was a brave and cunning god in the myths of Algonquian Native American people. He was a trickster who sometimes got tricked.

Guinevere (GWIHN uh vihr) in British and Welsh legends was King Arthur's queen, who was also loved by Sir Lancelot.

Gwydion (GWIHD ih uhn) in Welsh legends was the father of Llew and the nephew of the magician and ruler, Math.

H

Hades (HAY deez) in ancient Greece was the god of the dead. Hades was also called Pluto (PLOO toh). The Romans called him Dis.

Hairy Man was a frightening monster in African American folk tales.

Harpy (HAHRP ee) was one of the hideous winged women in Greek myths. The hero Jason and his Argonauts freed King Phineas from the harpies' power.

Hathor (HATH awr) was worshiped in the form of a cow in ancient Egypt, but she also appeared as an angry lioness. She was the daughter of Ra and the sister of Bastet and Sekhmet.

Heimdall (HAYM dahl) was the god in Norse myths who guarded the rainbow bridge joining Asgard, the home of the gods, to other worlds.

Hel (hehl), also called Hela, was the goddess of death in Norse myths. The lower half of her body was like a rotting corpse. Hel was Loki's daughter.

Helen (HEHL uhn), called Helen of Troy, was a real person in ancient Greece. According to legend, she was known as the most beautiful woman in the world. Her capture by Paris led to the Trojan War.

Heng E (huhng ay), sometimes called Chang E, was a woman in Chinese myths who became the moon goddess. She was the wife of Yi the Archer.

Hera (HEHR uh) in ancient Greece was the queen of heaven and the wife of Zeus. The Romans called her Juno.

Heracles (HEHR uh kleez) in ancient Greek myths was a hero of great strength. He was the son of Zeus. He had to complete twelve tremendous tasks in order to become one of the gods. The Romans called him Hercules.

Hermes (HUR meez) was the messenger of the gods in Greek myths. He wore winged sandals. The Romans called him Mercury.

Hoder (HOO dur) was Balder's twin brother in Norse myths. He was blind. It was said that after a mighty battle he and Balder would be born again.

Hoenir (HAY nihr), also called Honir, was a god in Norse myths. In some early myths, he is said to be Odin's brother.

Horus (HAWR uhs) in ancient Egypt was the son of Isis and Osiris. He was often shown with the head of a falcon. Horus fought Seth to rule Egypt.

Hreidmar (HRAYD mahr) was a dwarf king in Norse myths who held Odin for a huge pile of treasure. His sons were Otter, Fafnir, and Regin.

Hyrrokkin (HEER rahk kihn) in Norse myths was a terrifying female giant who rode an enormous wolf using poisonous snakes for reins.

I

Irin-Mage (eereen mah geh) in Tupinambá myths was the only person to be saved when the creator, Monan, destroyed the other humans. Irin-Mage became the ancestor of all people living today.

Isis (EYE sihs) in ancient Egypt was the goddess of fertility and a master of magic. She became the most powerful of all the gods and goddesses. She was the sister and wife of Osiris and mother of Horus.

J

Jade Emperor (jayd EHM puhr uhr) in Buddhist myths of China was the chief god in Heaven.

Jason (JAY suhn) was a hero in Greek myths. His ship was the Argo, and the men who sailed with him on his adventures were called the Argonauts.

Johnny Appleseed (AP uhl seed) was a real person, John Chapman. He is remembered in legends as the person who traveled across North America, planting apple orchards.

K

Kaboi (kah boy) was a very wise man in a Carajá myth. He helped his people find their way from their underground home to the surface of the earth.

Kewawkwuí (kay wow kwoo) were a group of powerful, frightening giants and magicians in the myths of Algonquian Native American people.

Kigbo (keeg boh) was a stubborn man in a Yoruba myth of Africa. His stubbornness got him into trouble with spirits.

Kodoyanpe (koh doh yahn pay) was a good god in the myths of the Maidu and some other Native American people. He was the brother of the evil god Coyote.

Kuang Zi Lian (kwahng dsee lee ehn) in a Taoist myth of China was a very rich, greedy farmer who was punished by one of the Eight Immortals.

Kui in Chinese myths was an ugly, brilliant scholar who became God of Examinations.

Kvasir (KVAH sihr) in Norse myths was the wisest of all the gods in Asgard.

L

Lancelot (lan suh laht) in British and Welsh legends was King Arthur's friend and greatest knight. He was secretly in love with Guinevere.

Lao Zi (low dzuh) was the man who founded the Chinese religion of Taoism. He wrote down the Taoist beliefs in a book, the *Tao Te Ching*.

Li Xuan (lee shwahn) was one of the Eight Immortals in ancient Chinese myths.

Light (lyt) was a child of Amma, the creator of the world, in a myth of the Dogon people of Africa.

Lizard (LIHZ urd) was an animal prince in an Alur myth of Africa. He was certain that he, and not his brother, Frog, would inherit the throne of their father.

Llew Llaw Gyffes (LE yoo HLA yoo GUHF ehs), also Lleu Law Gyffes, was a hero in Welsh myths who had many adventures. His mother was Arianrod and his father was Gwydion.

Loki (LOH kee) in Norse myths was a master trickster. His friends were Odin and Thor. Loki was half giant and half god, and could be funny and also cruel. He caused the death of Balder.

Lord of Heaven was the chief god in some ancient Chinese myths.

Lug (luk) in Irish myths was the Immortal High King of Ireland, Master of All Arts.

M

Maira-Monan (mah ee rah moh nahn) was the most powerful son of Irin-Mage in Tupinambá myths. He was destroyed by people who were afraid of his powers.

Manco Capac (mahn kih kah pahk) in Inca myths was the founder of the Inca people. He was one of four brothers and four sisters who led the Inca to their homeland.

Manitou (MAN ih toh) was the greatest and most powerful of all gods in Native American myths of the Iroquois people.

Math (mohth) in Welsh myths was a magician who ruled the Welsh kingdom of Gwynedd.

Michabo (mee chah boh) in the myths of Algonquian Native American people was the Great Hare, who taught people to hunt and brought them luck. He was a son of West Wind.

Monan (moh nahn) was the creator in Tupinambá myths.

Monkey (MUNG kee) is the hero of many Chinese stories. The most cunning of all monkeys, he became the king of monkeys and caused great troubles for the gods.

N

Nanook (na NOOK) was the white bear in myths of the Inuit people.

Naoise (NEE see) in Irish myths was Conchobar's nephew and the lover of Deirdre. He was the son of Usnech and brother of Ardan and Ainle.

Nekumonta (neh koo mohn tah) in Native American myths of the Iroquois people was a person whose goodness helped him save his people from a terrible sickness.

Nü Wa (nyuh wah) in a Chinese myth was a girl who, with her brother, Fu Xi, freed the Thunder God and was rewarded. Her name means Gourd Girl.

Nuada (NOO uh thuh) in Irish myths was King of the Tuatha Dé Danann, the rulers of all Ireland. He had a silver hand.

O

Odin (OH dihn), also called Woden, in Norse myths was the chief of all the gods and a brave warrior. He had only one eye. He was the husband of Frigga and father of many of the gods. His two advisers were the ravens Hugin and Munin.

Odysseus (oh DIHS ee uhs) was a Greek hero who fought in the Trojan War. The poet Homer wrote of his many adventures.

Oedipus (ED uh puhs) was a tragic hero in Greek myths. He unknowingly killed his own father and married his mother.

Olodumare (oh loh doo mah ray) was the supreme god in Yoruba myths of Africa.

Olokun (oh loh koon) was the god of water and giver of life in Yoruba myths of Africa. He challenged Olodumare for the right to rule.

Orpheus (AWR fee uhs) in Greek myths was famed for his music. He followed his wife, Euridice, to the kingdom of the dead to plead for her life.

Osiris (oh SY rihs) in ancient Egypt was the ruler of the dead in the kingdom of the West. He was the brother and husband of Isis and the father of Horus.

P

Pamola (pah moh lah) in the myths of Algonquian Native American people was an evil spirit of the night.

Pan Gu (pahn goo) in Chinese myths was the giant who was the first living being.

Pandora (pan DAWR uh) in ancient Greek myths was the first woman.

Paris (PAR ihs) was a real person, a hero from the city of Troy. He captured Helen, the queen of a Greek kingdom, and took her to Troy.

Paul Bunyan (pawl BUHN yuhn) was a tremendously strong giant lumberjack in North American myths.

Perseus (PUR see uhs) was a human hero in myths of ancient Greece. His most famous adventure was killing Medusa, a creature who turned anyone who looked at her to stone.

Poseidon (puh SY duhn) was the god of the sea in myths of ancient Greece. He carried a three-pronged spear called a trident to make storms and control the waves. The Romans called him Neptune.

Prometheus (pruh MEE thee uhs) was the cleverest of the gods in Greek myths. He was a friend to humankind.

Q

Queen Mother of the West was a goddess in Chinese myths.

R

Ra (rah), sometimes Re (ray), was the sun god of ancient Egypt. He was often shown with the head of a hawk. Re became the most important god. Other gods were sometimes combined with him and had Ra added to their names.

Ran (rahn) was the goddess of the sea in Norse myths. She pulled sailors from their boats in a large net and dragged them underwater.

Red Jacket in Chinese myths was an assistant to Wen Chang, the god of literature. His job was to help students who hadn't worked very hard.

S

Sekhmet (SEHK meht) in ancient Egypt was a blood-thirsty goddess with the head of a lioness. She was the daughter of Ra and the sister of Bastet and Hathor.

Setanta in Irish myths was Cuchulain's name before he killed the hound of Culan.

Seth (set), sometimes Set, in ancient Egypt was the god of chaos and confusion, who fought Horus to rule Egypt. He was the evil son of Geb and Nut.

Shanewis (shah nay wihs) in Native American myths of the Iroquois people was the wife of Nekumonta.

Shu (shoo) in ancient Egypt was the father of the sky goddess Nut. He held Nut above Geb, the Earth, to keep the two apart.

Sinchi Roca was the second emperor of the Inca. According to legend, he was the son of Ayar Manco (later known as Manco Capac) and his sister Mama Ocllo.

Skirnir (SKEER nihr) in Norse myths was a brave, faithful servant of the god Frey.

Sphinx (sfihngks) in Greek myths was a creature that was half lion and half woman, with eagle wings. It killed anyone who failed to answer its riddle.

T

Tefnut (TEHF noot) was the moon goddess in ancient Egypt. She was the sister and wife of Shu and the mother of Nut and Geb.

Theseus (THEE see uhs) was a human hero in myths of ancient Greece. He killed the Minotaur, a half-human, half-bull creature, and freed its victims.

Thor (thawr) was the god of thunder in Norse myths. He crossed the skies in a chariot pulled by goats and had a hammer, Mjollnir, and a belt, Meginjardir.

Thunder God (THUN dur gahd) in Chinese myths was the god of thunder and rain. He got his power from water and was powerless if he could not drink.

Tsui'goab (tsoo ee goh ahb) was the god of rain in myths of the Khoi people of Africa. He was a human who became a god after he fought to save his people.

Tupan (too pahn) was the spirit of thunder and lightning in Inca myths.

Tyr (tihr) was the god of war in Norse myths. He was the bravest god and was honorable and true, as well. He had just one hand.

U

Utgard-Loki (OOT gahrd LOH kee) in Norse myths was the clever, crafty giant king of Utgard. He once disguised himself as a giant called Skrymir to teach Thor a lesson.

W

Water God (WAW tur gahd) in Chinese myths was a god who sent rain and caused floods.

Wen Chang (wehn chuhng) in Chinese myths was the god of literature. His assistants were Kui and Red Jacket.

Wu (woo) was a lowly courtier in a Chinese myth who fell in love with a princess.

X

Xi He (shee heh) in Chinese myths was the goddess wife of Di Jun, the god of the eastern sky.

Xiwangmu (shee wahng moo) in Chinese myths was the owner of the Garden of Immortal Peaches.

Xuan Zang (shwahn dsahng), also called Tripitaka, was a real person, a Chinese Buddhist monk who traveled to India to gather copies of religious writings. Legends about him tell that Monkey was his traveling companion.

Y

Yan Wang (yahn wahng) was the god of the dead and judge of the first court of the Underworld in Chinese myths. He was helper to Di Zang Wang.

Yao (yow) was a virtuous emperor in Chinese myths. Because Yao lived simply and was a good leader, Yi the Archer was sent to help him.

Yi (yee) was an archer in Chinese myths who was sent by Di Jun to save the earth, in answer to Yao's prayers.

Z

Zeus (zoos) in ancient Greece was the king of gods and the god of thunder and lightning. The Romans called him Jupiter.

Zhao Shen Xiao (zhow shehn shi ow) in Chinese myths was a good magistrate, or official, who arrested the greedy merchant Kuang Zi Lian.

MYTHS AND LEGENDS GLOSSARY

This is a cumulative glossary of some important places and terms found in all eight volumes of the **World Book Myths and Legends** series.

A

Alfheim (AHLF hym) in Norse myth was the home of the light elves.

Asgard (AS gahrd) in Norse myths was the home of the warrior gods who were called the Aesir. It was connected to the earth by a rainbow bridge.

Augean (aw JEE uhn) stables were stables that the Greek hero Heracles had to clean as one of his twelve labors. He made the waters of two rivers flow through the stables and wash away the filth.

Avalon (AV uh lahn) in British legends was the island where King Arthur was carried after he died in battle. The legend says he will rise again to lead Britain.

B

Bard (bahrd) was a Celtic poet and singer in ancient times. A bard entertained people by making up and singing poems about brave deeds.

Battle of the Alamo (AL uh moh) was a battle between Texas settlers and Mexican forces when Texas was fighting for independence from Mexico. It took place at the Alamo, a fort in San Antonio, in 1836.

Bifrost (BEE fruhst) in Norse myths was a rainbow bridge that connected Asgard with the world of people.

Black Land in ancient Egypt was the area of fertile soil around the banks of the River Nile. Most people lived there.

Brer Rabbit (brair RAB iht) myths are African American stories about a rabbit who played tricks on his friends. The stories grew out of animal myths from Africa.

C

Canoe Mountain in a Maidu myth of North America was the mountain on which the evil Coyote took refuge from a flood sent to drown him.

Changeling (CHAYNG lihng) in Celtic myths was a fairy child who had been swapped with a human baby at birth. Changelings were usually lazy and clumsy.

Confucianism (kuhn FYOO shuhn IHZ uhm) is a Chinese way of life and religion. It is based on the teachings of Confucius, also known as Kong Fu Zi, and is more than 2,000 years old.

Creation myths (kree AY shuhn mihths) are myths that tell how the world began.

D

Dwarfs (dwawrfs) in Norse myths were small people of great power. They were skilled at making tools and weapons.

F

Fairies (FAIR eez) in Celtic myths were called the Little People. They are especially common in Irish legends, where they are called leprechauns.

Fomors (FOH wawrz) in Irish myths were hideous giants who invaded Ireland and were fought by Lug.

G

Giants (JY uhnts) in Norse myths were huge people who had great strength and great powers. They often struggled with the warrior gods of Asgard.

Gnome (nohm) was a small, odd-looking person in the myths of many civilizations. In Inca myths, for example, gnomes were tiny people with very big beards.

Golden Apples of the Hesperides (heh SPEHR uh deez) were apples of gold in a garden that only the Greek gods could enter. They were collected by the hero Heracles as one of his twelve labors.

Golden fleece was the fleece of a ram that the Greek hero Jason won after many adventures with his ship, Argo, and his companion sailors, the Argonauts.

Green Knoll (nohl) was the home of the Little People, or fairies, in Irish and Scottish myths.

J

Jotunheim (YUR toon hym) in Norse myths was the land of the giants.

L

Lion men in myths of Africa were humans who can turn themselves into lions.

Little People in Celtic legends and folk tales are fairies. They are often fine sword makers and blacksmiths.

M

Machu Picchu (MAH choo PEE choo) is the ruins of an ancient city built by the Inca in the Andes Mountains of Peru.

Medecolin (may day coh leen) were a tribe of evil sorcerers in the myths of Algonquian Native American people.

Medicine (MEHD uh sihn) **man** is a wise man or shaman who has special powers. Medicine men also appear as beings with special powers in myths of Africa and North and South America. Also see **Shaman.**

Midgard (MIHD gahrd) in Norse myths was the world of people.

Muspell (MOOS pehl) in Norse myths was part of the Underworld. It was a place of fire.

N

Nidavellir in Norse myths was the land of the dwarfs.

Niflheim in Norse myths was part of the Underworld. It included Hel, the kingdom of the dead.

Nirvana (nur VAH nuh) in the religion of Buddhism is a state of happiness that people find when they have freed themselves from wanting things. People who reach Nirvana no longer have to be reborn.

O

Oracle (AWRR uh kuhl) in ancient Greece was a sacred place served by people who could foretell the future. Greeks journeyed there to ask questions about their fortunes. Also see **Soothsayer.**

P

Pacariqtambo (pahk kah ree TAHM boh) in Inca myths was a place of three caves from which the first people stepped out into the world. It is also called Paccari Tampu.

Poppykettle was a clay kettle made for brewing poppy-seed tea. In an Inca myth, a poppykettle was used for a boat.

Prophecy (PRAH feh see) is a prediction made by someone who foretells the future.

R

Ragnarok (RAHG nah ruhk) in Norse myths was the final battle of good and evil, in which the giants would fight against the gods of Asgard.

S

Sahara (sah HAH rah) is a vast desert that covers much of northern Africa.

Seriema was a bird in a Carajá myth of South America whose call led the first people to try to find their way from underground to the surface of the earth.

Shaman (SHAH muhn) can be a real person, a medicine man or wise person who knows the secrets of nature. Shamans also appear as beings with special powers in some myths of North and South America. Also see **Medicine man.**

Soothsayer (sooth SAY ur) in ancient Greece was someone who could see into the future. Also see **Oracle.**

Svartalfheim (SVAHRT uhl hym) in Norse myths was the home of the dark elves.

T

Tar Baby was a sticky doll made of tar used to trap Brer Rabbit, a tricky rabbit in African American folk tales.

Tara (TAH rah) in Irish myths was the high seat, or ruling place, of the Irish kings.

Trickster (TRIHK stur) **animals** are clever ones that appear in many myths of North America, South America, and Africa.

Trojan horse. See **Wooden horse of Troy.**

Tuatha dÈ Danann (THOO uh huh day DUH nuhn) were the people of the goddess Danu. Later they were known as gods of Ireland themselves.

V

Vanaheim (VAH nah hym) in Norse myths was the home of the fertility gods.

W

Wadjet eye was a symbol used by the people of ancient Egypt. It stood for the eye of the gods Ra and Horus and was supposed to bring luck.

Wheel of Transmigration (tranz my GRAY shuhn) in the religion of Buddhism is the wheel people's souls reach after they die. From there they are sent back to earth to be born into a higher or lower life.

Wooden horse of Troy was a giant wooden horse built by the Greeks during the Trojan War. The Greeks hid soldiers in the horse's belly and left the horse for the Trojans to find.

Y

Yang (yang) is the male quality of light, sun, heat, and dryness in Chinese beliefs. Yang struggles with Yin for control of things.

Yatkot was a magical tree in an African myth of the Alur people.

Yggdrasil (IHG drah sihl) in Norse myths was a mighty tree that held all three worlds together and reached up into the stars.

Yin (yihn) is the female quality of shadow, moon, cold, and water in Chinese beliefs. Yin struggles with Yang for control of things.

CUMULATIVE INDEX

This is an alphabetical list of important topics covered in all eight volumes of the **World Book Myths and Legends** series. Next to each entry is at least one pair of numbers separated by a slash mark (/). For example, the entry for Argentina is "**Argentina** 8/4". The first number tells you what volume to look in for information. The second number tells you what page you should turn to in that volume. Sometimes a topic appears in more than one place. When it does, additional volume and page numbers are given. Here's a reminder of the volume numbers and titles: 1, *African Myths and Legends;* 2, *Ancient Egyptian Myths and Legends;* 3, *Ancient Greek Myths and Legends;* 4, *Celtic Myths and Legends;* 5, *Chinese Myths and Legends;* 6, *Norse Myths and Legends;* 7, *North American Myths and Legends;* 8, *South American Myths and Legends.*

A

Aeëtes, father of Medea 3/39–40
Aegeus, king of Athens 3/14, 3/15, 3/17
Aegir, god of the sea 6/5
African Americans 1/5, 7/2–3, 7/35–41, 8/4
African peoples 1/2–5
  see also under individual names, e.g., **Ashanti;**
  Khoi; Yoruba
Alamo, Battle of the 7/32
Alfheim, a Norse world 6/3
Algonquian peoples 7/4, 7/5, 7/7–9, 7/17–19
Alur myth 1/25–29
Amma, the creator 1/18–23
Amun, king of the gods 2/5
Andes, a mountain range 8/4, 8/31, 8/38
Andvari, a dwarf 6/14–15, 6/44
animal myths 1/19–23, 1/25–29, 1/43–47
  see also **trickster animals**
Antigone, daughter of Oedipus 3/47
Anubis, god of the dead 2/5, 2/17
Ao, a turtle 5/39–40
Aphrodite, goddess of love 3/4, 3/34
Appleseed, Johnny, a planter of trees 7/30–31
Ares, field of 3/39, 3/40
Argentina 8/4
Argo, Jason's ship 3/37–41
Argonauts see **Jason and the Argonauts**
Ariadne, daughter of Minos 3/15–17
Artemis, a goddess 3/26
Asare, a boy 8/43–47
Asgard, a Norse world 6/3, 6/4, 6/20, 6/22
Ashanti, an ancient African people 1/4
Asterion, king of Crete 3/13
Atalanta, the huntress 3/37
Athena, goddess of war 3/4, 3/9, 3/22, 3/27, 3/34, 3/35
Athenais, queen of Byblos 2/14–16
Atlas, holder of the heavens 3/28, 3/29
Atum, the creator god 2/4, 2/5
Augean stables 3/27

B

Babe, Paul Bunyan's pet ox 7/28–29
Balder, god of light 6/4, 6/35–39, 6/41–44
Ban Hu, a dog god 5/21–23
Bastet, the mother goddess 2/5
Bellerophon, a hero 3/5, 3/22–23
Benin, home of the Fon 1/4
Bifrost, a rainbow bridge 6/3, 6/5, 6/32
Black Land 2/2, 2/3, 2/4
Blodughofi, Frey's horse 6/26
Bolivia 8/4
Bororo, a South American people 8/3, 8/7–11
Botoque, the first human to eat cooked meat 8/13–17
Brazil 8/2
Brer Rabbit and the Tar Baby 1/5, 7/38–39
Brown Pelican, messenger to El Niño 8/38-39
Buddha and Buddhism 5/5, 5/25–29, 5/46–47
Bunyan, Paul, a lumberjack 7/26–29
bush spirits 1/4, 1/30–35

C

Caddo myth 7/44–47
Calusa, a North American people 7/4, 7/5
Canoe Mountain 7/46–47
Carajá, a South American people 8/3, 8/19–23
Carnarvon, Lord, British Egyptologist 2/3
Celts 4/2–5
Cerberus, guard dog of Tartarus 3/29
Ceryneian Hind, a deer 3/26
Chaga myth 1/37–41
chameleon, Olodumare's messenger 1/11
Chapman, John see **Appleseed, Johnny**
Cherokee, a North American people 7/4, 7/5
Chile 8/2, 8/4
Chimaera 3/22–23
China 5/2–5
Colombia 8/2
Columbus, Christopher 7/3
Communism 5/4
Confucianism 5/4, 5/19–23
Coyote, an evil god 7/42–47

creation myths 1/19–23, 2/4, 7/4, 7/7, 7/43
Creek, a North American people 7/4, 7/5
Cretan Bull 3/27
Crockett, Davy, a hunter 7/32–33
Crow, bringer of daylight 7/20–24
Cuzco, first Inca home 8/34, 8/35
Cyclopes, one-eyed giants 3/31–32

D

Daedalus, an inventor 3/14, 3/16, 3/20–21
death mask 1/3
death myth 1/13–17
Di Jun, God of the Eastern Sky 5/13, 5/16
Di Zang Wang, Lord of the Underworld 5/29
Dionysus, god of wine 3/3, 3/4, 3/7–8
dog myth 5/19–23
Dogon myth 1/19–23
Dolapo, Kigbo's wife 1/31–35
dragons 6/3, 6/16–17
Draupnir, a magic ring 6/26, 6/41, 6/43
Dromi, a special chain 6/21
dwarfs 6/5, 6/13–17, 6/21

E

Echo, a nymph 3/10–11
Ecuador 8/4
Egypt, Ancient 2/2–5
Eight Immortals, Chinese heroes 5/5, 5/31, 5/34–35
El Dorado, the Golden Man 8/5
El Niño, ruler of the wind, weather,
    and oceans 8/37, 8/38, 8/39, 8/41
envoy, an official of the pharaoh 2/37, 2/41
Epeius, a Trojan warrior 3/34
Erymanthian Boar 3/26, 3/27
Ethiope, a river 1/7
European settlers
    in North America 7/2–3, 7/4, 7/27–33
    in South America 8/2, 8/4
Eurydice, a nymph 3/33
Eurystheus, cousin of Heracles 3/25–29
exploration
    of Africa 1/3, 1/12
    of North America 7/2–3

F

Fafnir, a dwarf 6/5, 6/14, 6/16–17
famine 1/13
Fenris, a wolf 6/4, 6/19–23
fire
    the gift of 1/23
    the secret of 8/13, 8/15–17, 8/25–29
Fon, an ancient African people 1/4
Frey, god of summer 6/4, 6/25–27, 6/30
Freya, goddess of beauty 6/5, 6/30–31
Frigga, goddess wife of Odin 6/4, 6/35–37, 6/42, 6/43
Frog, a prince 1/24–29
Fu Xi, Gourd Boy 5/7–11

G

Gaunab, Death in human form 1/14–17
Geb, the Earth itself 2/5
Gerda, a giantess 6/25–27, 6/41

Geryon, a giant 3/28
Ghana, home of the Ashanti people 1/4
giants and giantesses 6/4, 6/5, 6/25–27, 6/41–42, 6/46
    see also **Cyclopes; Loki; Thrym; Utgard-Loki**
Gladsheim, a place of peace 6/35–36
Gleipnir, a magic rope 6/21–22
Glooskap, a god and trickster 7/16–19
gnomes 8/37, 8/41
gods and goddesses
    African 1/4
    ancient Egyptian 2/4–5
    ancient Greek 3/4–5
    Chinese 5/4, 5/5
    Norse 6/4–5
    North American 7/2, 7/4
    see also under individual names, e.g., **Amma;
        Coyote; Di Jun; Hera; Odin; Ra; Zeus**
gold 8/4, 8/5, 8/31
Golden Apples 3/28–29
Golden Fleece 3/37–41
Gorgons, monsters 3/9
Gourd Girl and Gourd Boy 5/7–11
gourds 1/36–41
Grand Canyon 7/29
grasslands 8/3, 8/19
Great Bear, a constellation 5/41
Greeks, ancient 3/2–3

H

Hades, god of the Underworld 3/4, 3/33
Hairy Man, a monster 7/34–37
Halley's comet 7/33
Harpies, curse of the 3/38
Harris, Joel Chandler, recorder of Brer Rabbit myths 7/38
Hathor, daughter of Ra 2/5, 2/26–29
Heimdall, a gatekeeper god 6/5, 6/32
Hel, goddess of death 6/4, 6/19, 6/42–44
Helen of Greece, later of Troy 3/5, 3/34–35
Helios, the sun god 3/19
Heng E, wife of Yi the Archer 5/15–17
Hera, goddess wife of Zeus 3/4, 3/25, 3/27, 3/28, 3/34
Heracles, hero son of Zeus 3/4, 3/19, 3/25–29, 3/37, 3/38
Hercules see **Heracles**
Hermes, messenger of the gods 3/4, 3/9
Hermod, messenger of the gods 6/42–43
heroes 3/2, 3/4–5, 3/34
    see also under individual names, e.g., **Eight Immortals;
        Heracles; Jason and the Argonauts; Theseus**
hieroglyphs 2/3
High Priest, serving Ra 2/28
Hippolyta, queen of the Amazons 3/28
Hlidskialf, a magic throne 6/4, 6/25
Hoder, god brother to Balder 6/4, 6/35, 6/37–39
Hoenir, god brother to Odin 6/5, 6/13–16
Homer 3/3
Horses of Diomedes 3/28
Horus, son of Osiris and Isis 2/2, 2/5, 2/19–23, 2/47
Hreidmar, a dwarf king 6/5, 6/13–16
Huanacauri, a mountain 8/32, 8/33
humankind, Ra's destruction of 2/25–29
Hydra, the many-headed monster 3/26
Hyrrokkin, a giantess 6/5, 6/41–42

I

Icarus, son of Daedalus 3/20–21
Iguana Islands, home of the dragon lizards 8/40
Iliad, The 3/3
Inca, a South American people 8/3–5, 8/31–35, 8/37–41
Indians, American see **North American peoples**
Inuit, a North American people 7/5, 7/21–24
Iobates, king of Lycia 3/22–23
Iolas, cousin of Heracles 3/26
Irin-Mage, father of humankind 8/26–27
Iroquois, a North American people 7/11–15
Isis, goddess of fertility 2/5, 2/7–11, 2/21–23
   discovering Ra's secret name 2/43–47
   search for Osiris 2/13–17

J

Jade Emperor 5/45, 5/46
jaguar 8/13, 8/15–17
James I, King of England 8/5
Jason and the Argonauts 3/5, 3/37–41
jatoba, a tree 8/15, 8/46–47
Jocasta, queen of Thebes 3/43, 3/46–47
Jormungand, a serpent 6/3, 6/10–11, 6/19
Jotunheim, a Norse world 6/3

K

Ka, Island of 2/37–41
Kaboi, a very wise man 8/19, 8/23
Kayapó a South American people 8/3, 8/13–17
Kewawkqu', a race of giants and magicians 7/17
Khoi, an African people 1/13–17
Kigbo, a stubborn man 1/30–35
Knossos, palace of 3/14
Kodoyanpe, brother god of Coyote 7/43–46
Kuang Zi Lian, a rich merchant and farmer 5/31–35
Kui, an ugly scholar 5/37–41
Kvasir, a wise god 6/5, 6/44–47

L

Labors of Heracles 3/25–29
Labyrinth, of Daedalus 3/14–17, 3/20
Laeding, a special chain 6/20
Laius, king of Thebes 3/43–47
Lao Zi, founder of Taoism 5/5, 5/46
Li Xuan, one of the Eight Immortals 5/34–35
Light, child of Amma 1/18–20, 1/22, 1/23
lion men 1/42–47
Lizard, a prince 1/24–29
Loki, half giant, half god 6/4, 6/19
   Andvari's ring 6/13–16
   Balder's death 6/36–38
   his downfall 6/44–47
   in the land of the giants 6/7, 6/8, 6/10
   stolen hammer myth 6/29–33
Lord of Heaven 5/10

M

Ma'at, goddess of justice 2/45
macaw, a clever bird 8/7–10, 8/13–15
Machu Picchu, an ancient Inca city 8/38
Maidu myth 7/43–47

Maira-Monan, son of Irin-Mage 8/27–29
Mali myths 1/19–23, 1/43–47
Manco Capac, founder of the Inca 8/35
Manitou, an Iroquois god 7/12–14
Medea, daughter of King Aeëtes 3/39–41
Medecolin, a race of cunning sorcerers 7/17
medicine man 1/43–47
Medusa, the Gorgon 3/9, 3/22
Meginjardir, a magic belt 6/4, 6/7
Melcarthus, king of Byblos 2/14, 2/16
Mi Hun Tang, the Potion of Forgetting 5/26
Michabo, the Great Hare 7/6–9
Midas, king of Phrygia 3/7–8
Midgard, a Norse world 6/3, 6/9, 6/29
Minos, king of Crete 3/13–16, 3/20
Minotaur, half man, half bull 3/13–17, 3/20
missionaries 1/3
mistletoe trick 6/35–39
Mjollnir, Thor's magic hammer 6/4, 6/7, 6/29–33, 6/37, 6/42
Modgurd, a gatekeeper 6/42–43
Monan, Tupinamba creator god 8/25–27
Monkey, the most cunning of all monkeys 5/43–47
murder of Osiris 2/7–11
Muspell, a Norse world 6/3

N

Nanna, goddess wife of Balder 6/38, 6/42
Nanook, the white bear 7/23
Narcissus, a man who loved himself 3/10–11
Narve, son of Loki 6/46
Native American peoples see **North American peoples;**
   South American peoples
Neith, mother of Ra 2/23
Nekumonta, the Iroquois brave 7/10–15
Nemean lion 3/25
Nephthys, wife of Seth 2/17
Nidavellir, a Norse world 6/3
Nidhogg, a dragon 6/3
Niflheim, a Norse world 6/3, 6/19, 6/42–43
Niger, a river 1/46
Nigeria, home of the Yoruba 1/3, 1/4
Nile River 2/2
nirvana, a blissful state 5/5
Norse people 6/2–5
North American peoples 7/2–5
   native 7/2–5, 7/7–25, 7/43–47
   see also **African Americans; European settlers;**
   and individual tribes, e.g., **Inuit; Iroquois; Sioux**
Nu, a god 2/25–26
Nü Wa, Gourd Girl 5/7–11
Nut, the sky goddess 2/5
nymphs 3/9, 3/10–11, 3/33, 3/38

O

ochre, very red earth 2/27–29
Odin, chief of the gods 6/4, 6/25, 6/39, 6/41
   Andvari's ring 6/13–16
   downfall of Loki 6/44–47
   trapping the wolf, Fenris 6/19–22
Odysseus, a hero 3/3, 3/5, 3/31–32, 3/34
Odyssey, The 3/3

Oedipus, a tragic hero 3/5, 3/43–47
Olodumare, the supreme god 1/7–11
Olokun, god of the sea 1/6–11
Olympus, Mount, home of the gods 3/4, 3/19, 3/23, 3/25, 3/29
oracles 3/14, 3/44, 3/46
Orpheus, husband of Eurydice 3/5, 3/33
Osiris, ruler of the dead 2/5
   murder of 2/7–11
   search for 2/13–17

P

Pacariqtambo, the place of origin 8/31, 8/33, 8/35
Pamola, evil spirit of the night 7/17
Pan Gu, the first living being 5/43
Pandora, the first woman 3/5, 3/43
papyrus 2/3
Paris, a Trojan hero 3/5, 3/34–35
Pasiphaë, wife of King Minos 3/14
Pegasus, the winged horse 3/22–23
Periboea, queen of Corinth 3/44, 3/46
Persephone, wife of Hades 3/33
Perseus, a hero 3/4, 3/9, 3/22
Peru 8/2, 8/4, 8/31, 8/37
pharaohs, rulers of Egypt 2/2, 2/31–35
Phineus, soothsayer king of Thrace 3/38–39
Poetic Edda, a collection of stories 6/2–3
Polybus, king of Corinth 3/44, 3/46
Polyphemus, the Cyclops 3/31–32
Poppykettle, a sailing vessel 8/37, 8/39–41
Poseidon, god of the sea 3/4, 3/13, 3/14, 3/31
Priam, king of Troy 3/34
Proitos, king of Argos 3/22, 3/23
Prometheus, a god 3/4, 3/19, 3/28
Prose Edda, a collection of stories 6/2
pyramids of Egypt 2/2

Q

Queen Mother of the West, a goddess 5/16

R

Ra, the sun god 2/2, 2/4, 2/5, 2/7, 2/17, 2/20
   destruction of humankind 2/25–29
   secret name 2/43–47
Ragnarok, final battle 6/4, 6/23, 6/27, 6/47
Raleigh, Sir Walter, an English explorer 8/5
Ran, goddess of the sea 6/5
   net used by Loki 6/15, 6/44
Ratatosk, a squirrel 6/3
Red Jacket, assistant to the God of Literature 5/40–41
Regin, a dwarf 6/5, 6/14, 6/16
religion 1/3, 5/4–5, 8/2, 8/25
Rhampsinitus, a rich pharaoh 2/31–35
Ringhorn, a longboat 6/41, 6/42
Romans, ancient 3/3

S

Sahara 1/2
sailor myth 2/37–41
savanna 8/19, 8/20
secret name of Ra 2/43–47
Sekhmet, daughter of Ra 2/5
seriema, a bird 8/19, 8/20, 8/21, 8/23
serpents 6/10–11, 6/46–47
Seth, god of chaos 2/5, 2/8–11, 2/16–17, 2/19–23
shamans 7/4, 7/44–45, 8/27, 8/28
Shanewis, wife of Nekumonta 7/10–15
Sherente, a South American people 8/3, 8/43–47
shipwreck myth 2/37–41
Shu, father of Nut 2/5, 2/19
Sigurd, a dwarf 6/17
Sigyn, goddess wife of Loki 6/47
silk 5/3
Sinchi Roca, second emperor of the Inca 8/34, 8/35
Sioux, a North American people 7/25
Skadi, a giantess 6/46
Skirnir, a servant 6/5, 6/21–22, 6/25–27
slavery 1/5, 7/2, 7/3, 7/39, 7/40–41
snake meat 7/25
snake myths 2/38–41, 2/44–46
Snorri Sturluson, Icelandic author 6/2–3
soothsayers 3/7, 3/38–39, 3/46, 3/47
souls, land of the 1/6–7
South African myth 1/13–17
South American peoples 8/2–5
   see also under individual groups, e.g., **Inca;**
      Kayapó; Sherente
Spanish conquest of South America 8/5, 8/37, 8/38
Sphinx, half lion, half woman 3/45–46
spirit of the mountain 1/37–38, 1/40
stars, the creation of 8/7–11
Stymphalian Birds 3/27
sun gods 2/4, 8/5
   see also **Ra**
Svartalfheim, land of dark elves 6/3
Symplegades Rocks 3/38, 3/39

T

Talos, nephew of Daedalus 3/20–21
tamarisk tree 2/14, 2/15
Taoism 5/5, 5/31–35
Tar Baby see **Brer Rabbit and the Tar Baby**
Tartarus, the Underworld 3/29, 3/33
Tata, a terrible fire from heaven 8/26
Tefnut, a moon goddess 2/5
Teiresias, a soothsayer 3/46, 3/47
Theseus, a hero 3/4, 3/15–17, 3/20
Thialfi, a servant 6/7, 6/8, 6/10
Thor, god of thunder 6/4, 6/36, 6/37, 6/38
   downfall of Loki 6/44–47
   in the land of giants 6/7–11
   stolen hammer myth 6/29–33
Thrym, a giant 6/30–33
Thunder God 5/7–10
Tree of Life 6/3
trickster animals 1/5, 8/4

Tsui'goab, the rain god 1/12–17
Tupan, the spirit of thunder and lightning 8/29
Tupinambá, a South American people 8/3, 8/25–29
Tutankhamen, pharaoh of Egypt 2/3
Tyr, god of war 6/4, 6/19–23

U

Underworld myths 5/25–29, 5/44–45
Utgard-Loki, a giant 6/5, 6/7–11, 6/37, 6/41

V

Vali, god son of Odin 6/39
Vali, son of Loki 6/46
Valley of the Kings 2/2, 2/3
Vanaheim, a Norse world 6/3
Vikings 6/2, 6/5

W

wadjet eye 2/2
Wasis, a mighty baby 7/16–19
Water, child of Amma 1/18–20, 1/22, 1/23
Water God 5/10
Wen Chang, God of Literature 5/39–41
Wheel of Transmigration 5/26
Wiley, a little boy who tricked the Hairy Man 7/34–37
Woden see **Odin**

wolves 6/19–23, 6/41–42
wooden horse of Troy 3/34–35
Wu, a lowly courtier in love with a princess 5/19–23

X

Xi He, goddess wife of Di Jun 5/13–15
Xiwangmu, Queen of the West 5/45
Xuan Zang, a Buddhist monk, 5/43, 5/47

Y

Yan Wang, judge of the first court of the Underworld 5/29
yang, the male hot sun 5/13, 5/17
Yao, an Emperor 5/15–16
yatkot, a magic tree 1/26–27
"Year of the Dog" myth 5/19–23
Yggdrasil, Tree of Life 6/3
Yi, the Archer 5/13, 5/15–17
yin, the female cold moon 5/13, 5/17
Yoruba, an ancient African people 1/3, 1/4, 1/7–11, 1/31–35

Z

Zeus, king of the gods 3/4, 3/11, 3/19, 3/23, 3/25, 3/28
Zhao Shen Xiao, a good magistrate 5/32, 5/34–35

ISBN(set): 0-7166-2613-6
African Myths and Legends
ISBN: 0-7166-2605-5
LC: 2001026492

Ancient Egyptian Myths and Legends
ISBN: 0-7166-2606-3
LC: 2001026501

Ancient Greek Myths and Legends
ISBN: 0-7166-2607-1
LC: 2001035959

Celtic Myths and Legends
ISBN: 0-7166-2608-X
LC: 20011026496

Chinese Myths and Legends
ISBN: 0-7166-2609-8
LC: 2001026489

Norse Myths and Legends
ISBN: 0-7166-2610-1
LC: 2001026488

North American Myths and Legends
ISBN: 0-7166-2611-X
LC: 2001026490

South American Myths and Legends
ISBN: 0-7166-2612-8
LC: 2001026491